ENDORSEMENTS FOR JOHNNY VIC

~~~*"Johnny Vic's adventures are a fun way to enjoy and get kids excited about history."*

> **--Mike Austin, Ph.D., Project Director of Teaching American History, Castleton State College.**

~~~*"My students love the Johnny Vic stories and I value the way real information is woven into exciting adventures– it's an easy way for children to learn history."*

> **--Pam Hunter, 6th Grade Teacher, Wells Village School.**

*Happy Reading...
Don't forget to visit my Website!*

Ann Rick Duncan

Johnny Vic's NAUTICAL ADVENTURES

A METALS OF TIME HISTORICAL FANTASY SERIES
BY ANN RICH DUNCAN

INFINITY
PUBLISHING.COM

ABOUT THE AUTHOR

Ann Rich Duncan is the author of *The Seed,* a top-ten finalist in the New Century Writers' Awards–a contemporary story that she describes as a cozy novel of suspense that warns us about the dangerous path we are traveling in regard to our food supply. Duncan is also the creator and author of this *Johnny Vic adventure series.* The inspiration for Johnny Vic? Her brother, a real treasure hunter based in Alaska. Duncan is also an artist and creator of original inspirational cards and framed prints. Visit her website at www.annrichduncan.com.

Johnny Vic's Nautical Adventures

by Ann Rich Duncan

Other books by Ann Rich Duncan

Travel With Johnny Vic
(Infinity Publishing)
ISBN# 0-7414-2315-4

The SEED
(Infinity Publishing)
ISBN# 0-7414-3072-X

A *Metals of Time* Historical Fantasy Series
By Ann Rich Duncan

Champlain Gold

Wow! Johnny Vic witnesses the Battle of Valcour
and he discovers a fortune in gold while he's there.
But will he be able to find it again
when he returns to his own century?

Columbus!

Christopher Columbus was a cagey one! He used
the eclipse of the moon to save his men;
and Johnny Vic got to see him do it!

Written by Ann Rich Duncan
research by Bill Clark and Dr. William Herman Bloom

ISBN 0-7414-5348-7

Published by:

INFIɷITY
PUBLISHING.COM

1094 New DeHaven Street, Suite 100
West Conshohocken, PA 19428-2713
Info@buybooksontheweb.com
www.buybooksontheweb.com
Toll-free (877) BUY BOOK
Local Phone (610) 941-9999
Fax (610) 941-9959

Printed in the United States of America

Published June 2009

ACKNOWLEDGMENTS

Mega THANKS! To all those individuals who helped to make this second book in the Johnny Vic series happen–especially to John Victor Pulling, the inspiration for the Johnny Vic character. Thanks also extended to Dr. William H. Bloom and Bill Clark (descriptions listed below) who shared their extensive knowledge of history. Special thanks also to Eric Smeltzer, scientist and water quality expert who filled in the facts about phosphorus and the pollution problems in Lake Champlain, and to Linda Knowlton, Sue Clark, Bill Clark and Dr. Bloom for agreeing to be characters in the stories along with our good friend, Dick Knowlton, who lost his valiant battle with cancer before the book was published. And of course, it goes without saying, that this author's spouse, Don, has been mega super throughout the process.

Dr. William Herman Bloom is a retired neurosurgeon, published author, poet and playwright who shared his extensive knowledge of and passion for Christopher Columbus. Dr. B provided several of the 'plots' in *COLUMBUS!*. He has collected many distinctions as an author, garnering a Pulitzer nomination in letters for his book, *Wit, Wisdom and Whimsy*, and is a prize-winning poet; a scientist with contributions in the field of neuroimmunology and clinical neuroscience. Dr. Bloom was also elected to Who's Who in American Health Care, and Who's Who in Science and Engineering. He was an authority on the complications of head injury, reviewing books on neural trauma for the prestigious Journal of Neurosurgery.

Bill Clark shared his own passion and expertise on the subject of Lake Champlain. A farmer and local civic leader, he is the author of *Lake Champlain, the Sixth Great Lake.* A prolific commentator, his articles have been published in many periodicals throughout the country.

Special Thanks
to Dover Publications, Inc.
for the use of the Johnny Vic silhouette chosen from:
Silhouettes: A Pictorial Archive of Varied Illustrations

This Book is dedicated to the memory of Richard Knowlton

***

Champlain Gold!

A Johnny Vic Adventure

by
Ann Rich Duncan

Chapter 1

The one that got away!

Johnny Vic peered upwards toward a noisy flock of seagulls. With one hand clutching his fishing pole and the other shading his eyes from the bright sunlight, he watched three of the feathered creatures squabble over their favorite perch–a thin, wooden pole at the end of the dock. The birds bickered and bounced and fluttered and flounced until one of them won its chance to settle upon the pole. It squawked triumphantly and the others quickly soared toward the rocky end of the beach. Johnny wondered if there were rules to this daily ritual that he dubbed, 'the bossy bird's proud perch game.' It always ended with the losers flying to the rocks. *It's like they've been banished from their favorite fishing spot,* he thought.

A large boat sounded its horn and soon Johnny Vic was bracing himself against the gentle sway of the dock as the lazy waves lapped at the pilings beneath him. High overhead, puffy white clouds eased their way southward. Johnny Vic studied them.

"Hey, Uncle Ben," he said. "One of those clouds looks like a dog with his tongue hanging out–can you see it?"

Ben looked heavenward.

"You're right, kiddo–I see it. Looks like Lucas, don't you think?"

Ben took a deep breath and reveled at the panoramic scenery. Lake Champlain stretched as far as the eye could see toward the north and south. Across the lake, the gorgeous fall foliage of Vermont, the Green Mountain State, etched a colorful path along the eastern edge of the Champlain basin.

As he often did, Ben uttered an oath of thanks to his Creator for days like this. *And for projects like this,* he thought. *Here I am, fishing and swimming, boating and diving–and it's part of my job!*

BENJAMIN VICTOR BRADLEY was a well-known author and journalist who had recently been hired to write a lengthy feature story about Lake Champlain. He planned to reveal the life of the lake, from 1609 when Samuel de Champlain made his famous discovery of the pristine waterway, to its not-so-pristine existence today. He had leased a cabin on the New York shore, and as he often did, he had invited his nephew, Johnny Vic, to join him. Thoughts of the boy prompted him to glance once again toward the north side of the dock.

With a crooked smile, Ben said, "Looks like you're just a bit tangled there, kiddo! Need some help with your line?"

"Nope. I can get it . . . I think." Johnny's cheeks burned, but his eyes sparkled with humor.

"Okay," Ben said, "but I'm here if you need me." He secured his bait, then gracefully cast his line southward. Within nano-seconds the line snapped tight and the tip of his pole quivered with angry jerks. He exclaimed, "Hey! I got one already, Johnny Vic!"

The boy dropped his own fishing pole and hopped across the warm wooden planks to watch. "Wow, it looks like it could be a big one, Uncle Ben!"

"Yup!"

"I hope you catch him . . . hey, why is your reel

squealing like that?"

"It's designed to give a little so I don't yank the hook out of his mouth–you know what I mean, Aboline?"

"Yuppy yup, Buttercup."

Johnny Vic dropped to his knees. "Hey, he's giving quite a fight!" The taught line slashed through the water as the frenzied fish dashed this way and that. Johnny Vic sucked in a gallon of air when the fish suddenly stopped struggling. *Has the fish given up?* he wondered as he watched Ben carefully reel it in. With a happy grin, Ben plopped to his own knees and reached down to retrieve his catch.

Unfortunately, the fish had other ideas. It gave a mighty flop and pulled itself free.

"Oh no! He got away!"

"That's okay, kiddo. I'll hook another one sooner or later. He did put up a pretty good fight, though, don't you think?"

"He sure did, but I bet you get a bigger one the next time, Uncle Ben, and I bet he'll be a record breaker, too."

Ben gave his nephew a soft tap on the shoulder and said, "I like how you think." Then he glanced at his watch. "Oh, oh. We'd better go back to the cabin and grab some lunch. Eric will be here soon."

Ben reeled in the fishless hook and asked, "Are you ready to go, Bongo Joe?"

"Yessiree, Boogie-Dee . . . soon as I get my line free."

"Here. Take my knife."

"Thanks."

***

Chapter 2

Clean and Clear

Eric Smeltzer was an environmental scientist who was working on the State of Vermont's program to clean up the water in Lake Champlain. He was the first person Ben had spoken to when he began making contacts in Vermont and he had proved to be very helpful. He arrived at the cabin just as Johnny Vic was stuffing the last bite of his sandwich into his mouth. *Way to go, guy,* he thought. *Uncle Ben won't want to do the dishes now that you're here . . . .*

But Johnny Vic's musings were rudely interrupted when Ben said, "Hey, Eric! Good to see you again. Take a seat while we clear up this mess."

"Arrgggh!"

Ben ignored Johnny Vic's groan and said, "Want a cold drink, Eric? Or a coffee?"

"I'd love a cold one, Ben."

"Okay, well, let's see. We've got iced tea and a few sodas in the fridge here. And some cups are getting frosty in the freezer–help yourself."

"Thanks."

"By the way, this young lad here is my nephew, Johnny Vic."

4

Eric shook Johnny Vic's hand, then he chose a Ginger Ale and a large frosty goblet with an emblem that read, "Go Red Sox." As he poured his drink it bubbled and hissed and formed a frothy head. He took a quick sip, then said, "I saw the governor yesterday. He's really glad you're doing this story. Good press for the lake, you know. And for the state. Too bad you couldn't get a cabin on the Vermont side, though."

"Hey, that's okay. Actually, I have clear view of Vermont from here. Helps to keep me inspired."

Ben raised his brows for emphasis and added, "I hope the Gov will be happy with what I do with this story."

"I'm sure he will. He saw your story about Calvin Coolidge and he loved it." Eric took another sip and chose a seat with a view of the lake, but he turned toward his host. "So, what do you want to start with? My schedule is fairly flexible." His round brown eyes remained wide with question.

"Well, we've spent the last three days just enjoying the lake. Getting the feel for the fishing and boating. We've been out in the little dinghy, touring the shoreline, so I guess I'm ready to spend some time just shadowing you, if that's okay."

"Of course."

"So tell me about your work, Eric. Do you test the water yourself? Have you seen any progress with your efforts to control the pollution?"

"Well, to answer your first question, I do go out in the field, sometimes–to get samples and to see for myself what's going on with the fish and plants. But, as you know, a lot of my work is done right in the office with a computer and telephone."

Eric took a quick sip of his soda, then continued. "But don't worry–I've arranged for a friend of mine to show you his work, too. I'm sure you know about the schooner the museum built awhile back? The Lake Champlain Maritime Museum?"

"Of course. You're talking about the Lois McClure,

5

right?"

"That's the one. He's offered to take you on a dive to see one of the sunken schooners it was based on–if you're interested."

Johnny Vic's eyes registered amazement. "You talking about diving–like in scuba diving?"

"You got it, kid."

"Wow! Uncle Ben, can you really scuba dive?"

"I sure can. As soon as I nailed this assignment I took lessons." He looked at Eric. "I can't wait to see that boat!"

"What kind of boat is it?" Johnny Vic asked.

"Well, for starters, no matter what else you do or say, please don't call it a 'boat' in front of the guys. It's a schooner. The original sailing canal schooners carried cargo in the 1800's. The one you'll be diving to, sank to the bottom of the lake in the mid 1800's. The museum hired a maritime archeologist to check a couple of them out; and, well, his sketches and descriptions were so accurate they hatched the plan to build a replica. They've sailed it down the lake and into the canal a few times already."

"Neat! Will we get to see it?"

"You'll do more than see it, Johnny Vic. You'll get a chance to sail on it–if your uncle agrees to go on the trip."

"To be honest, Eric, I've already been in touch with the museum. I haven't mentioned it to my nephew because I wanted it to be a surprise."

Ben looked at Johnny Vic. "Your Mom already knows about it and she said to go for it–so you can come, too! Apparently, your teacher said you could afford to miss a few days of school."

"Awesome!"

"But . . . she wants a written report. She knows we'll be spending time with scientists like Eric, and going to sites like the Lake Champlain Maritime Museum, so you'll have to include some science and some history in your writeup."

Ben tapped Johnny Vic's arm. "So . . . do you want to go Koko-Mo? We're leaving Monday."

"Yippee!"

In his excitement, Johnny Vic forgot their name game. He simply sputtered, "Thank you, thank you, thank you! You're the bestest, the neatest, the most awesomest uncle in the whole wide world!"

* * *

Chapter 3

Yuck, phosphorus!

What's phosphorus got to do with Lake Champlain? Johnny Vic wondered. He had been daydreaming about old schooners and explorers like Samuel de Champlain and had not been following the conversation. Eric had just explained that phosphorus is a fertilizing nutrient for plants that makes the lake soupy green with algae when there is too much of it.

"Phosphorus in the lake?" Johnny Vic asked. "How'd it get there? Can't you stop people from putting it into it?"

"Well, Johnny, to be honest, there are so many ways that phosphorus gets into the water, we can't blame any one person. There's point sources, like industrial discharges and wastewater treatment–you know, like pipes and sewer lines? Then you have non-point sources–like runoff–from roads, lawns, gardens, and other places like that. Although most people usually think about big business and factories when they think about pollution, the truth is, about 90-percent of the phosphorus comes to the lake from those non-point areas. Actually, it can come from dozens of miles away."

"How does it get there from so far away–wouldn't it dissolve in the dirt first?"

"Phosphorus doesn't break down like some forms of

pollution. It just gets carried along." Eric's forehead wrinkled with a new thought. He looked at Johnny Vic and asked, "You know how I mentioned the farms?"

"Yes . . . ."

"Well, any garden could add to the problem. Let's say there's a street in a small town in Vermont. It could be miles away from the lake. And on that street there are six small vegetable gardens and several lawns. Every landowner dumps fertilizer on his lawn or garden, year after year. Some of it runs into the gutter, or into a nearby stream. Maybe the stream dumps into a larger one, or directly into the lake. Wherever it goes, if it's within the Champlain basin, it's on a journey that eventually brings the phosphorus to the lake. And the Champlain basin encompasses some 8-thousand-200 square miles, you know."

ERIC CONTINUED to explain that phosphorus and algae levels were high in several parts of Lake Champlain, including Missisquoi Bay, St. Albans Bay and the South Lake area.

"So, I guess it's hard to blame somebody."

"Exactly. But, I don't like the word, 'blame.' For a very long time our farmers didn't know what they were doing to the lake–no one did for that matter–and now that they know, they can't afford to change how they do things. At least not right away." He shrugged. "Farmers take a beating these days. It's a hard enough life . . . without us environmental wackos coming down on them."

Ben grinned. "You definitely are not an environmental wacko, Eric."

"I know. But, it's hard to avoid that label. At any rate, I'm hoping we can do more to help them keep the phosphorus out of the lake. Like I said, many of them want to make the changes, but they just can't afford it. At least, not now."

"So how can they get help?"

"That's a good question, Johnny Vic. And, actually, one way is with the Clean and Clear Water Plan the governor put into place. There's money there to help the farmers, but I'm afraid it isn't enough." Eric clapped his hands together prayer fashion and raised his eyes toward the ceiling.

"We're doing everything we can! And now, with the 400th anniversary celebrations, we've got even more pressure on us to get that lake cleaned up." He jumped to his feet and trained his eyes on his host. "I hope your article will help our cause, Ben."

"I hope so, too, Eric. I hope so, too." Ben gazed out the window. He saw an expanse of white caps. "Hey, the wind's kicked up a notch."

"Supposed to be a cracker jack of a thunder storm tonight," Eric said.

"Darn!" Johnny Vic muttered, "I was hoping we could go fishing again tonight."

Ben said, "Hey, the fishing's usually better after a storm . . . and that's a fact, Master Jack."

"Yeah? Really? I hope so, Gee-eye-Joe."

"Just watch and see, Baggy-Dee."

"I'll do just that, Benny-Cat."

Eric watched their silly exchange with raised brows and a big grin.

"SO ERIC, WANT TO come to dinner tomorrow night? I'm having some friends over. I'm sure you'd like to meet them."

"Sure. Who's coming?"

"Bill and Sue Clark. He's a farmer who's had an interest in the lake and its history for a long time and his wife, Sue, makes awesome breads and jellies. And Dick and Linda Knowlton are coming, too. Linda's an old friend of mine–a real organizer. I bet they'd all like to help to promote this big puddle and get it cleaned up."

"Puddle?"

Ben laughed and ushered his friend toward his car. "Sorry, chum. After all, Champ wouldn't live in a puddle now, would he?"

"Champ? Who's Champ?"

"I'll tell you all about Champ at bed time–all righty, Mighty-Tykey?"

"It'll be a tale, Jabber-dale!"

"Do you two always do that?"

"Do what?" Johnny Vic and Ben exclaimed in unison.

Eric shook his head and jumped into his car. He hoped that his sister's baby would be just like Johnny Vic. *This kid's a corker,* he thought as he lowered his window and exclaimed, "See you later, alligator!"

***

Chapter 4

Gobs of Gook!

Johnny Vic was content to sit and listen. He was sleepy after having his fill of broasted chicken, corn-on-the-cob and potato salad. *Not to mention Sue's famous Maple Raisin Nut Bread,* he thought. *Oh, and the peanut butter cookies that Linda's friend sent. Man, they were good!* Johnny Vic had never been interested in recipes–but he was determined to get that one. He made a mental note to ask Linda about it. *Later,* he thought as he drifted off to sleep.

Ben smiled when his nephew slumped against his shoulder. They were on the cushiony settee in the camp. *This is so cozy, I might fall asleep, too,* he thought. But he didn't. His guests were talking about Lake Champlain and he was amazed at the amount of knowledge that seemed to flow from Bill Clark's brain. *He's a smart guy,* Ben thought. *I wonder if he'll show me what he's written about the lake– might be helpful. Real helpful.* Ben shifted to a more comfortable position and propped Johnny Vic's head on a pillow on his lap as he listened. Bill was telling Eric some of his own colorful tales about Lake Champlain.

" . . . Tough thing is, Eric, the lake's been in trouble for a long time. Why, I remember seeing these gray globs of gunk just floating in the lake. And tar, for heaven's sake! Tar would wash up on the shore just south of Ticonderoga. Black, sticky stuff that clung to the rocks and rotten branches. Why, sometimes we'd have to walk a mile or so, just to find access to the lake where we wouldn't get our shoes all mucked up with the sticky stuff. And that–Eric–was way back in the early sixties for cryin' out loud."

"I know. You're not the first person to tell me about it. It just boggles my mind."

"Boggle–that's a good word for it, Eric. I guess you could say we were boggled in glop."

***

Chapter 5

Shucks! He sees me!

The sun was almost ready to make an appearance. It was still dark. *Dark and quiet and spooky,* Johnny Vic thought. It was as if the earth was holding its breath, waiting for the sun to appear–and then the wind would once again blow and the birds would chirp and the dewdrops would glisten.

Johnny Vic fell to his knees on the sandy beach and slipped his bulging backpack underneath a bright red canoe. It was filled with supplies, including: a flashlight and extra batteries, a length of rope, a hammer and nails, some food, a sturdy knife, a blanket, and extra clothing. He was going to be prepared for anything on his next adventure.

Johnny Vic stood back and studied the upturned boat from several angles. *I gotta be sure Uncle Ben doesn't see my stuff.* Once he was convinced that his secret was safe, he scurried back toward the cabin. The sun was already visible and two chickadees were chattering at him from nearby branches.

Chick-a-dee-dee-dee!" he whispered back at them and grinned when they flittered closer.

I MADE IT! NOBODY knows a thing! Johnny Vic

thought as he slipped through his bedroom door. He tiptoed toward his bed and was quietly pulling his shoes off when he finally realized that he was wrong. Someone was quite aware of his early morning trek.

"Umh, hi, Dick."

"Hello, Johnny Vic."

"So, umh . . . whatcha' doin'?"

"I'm just wondering what you are doing."

"Me?"

"Yes, you."

"I, umh, I umh . . . I was looking at the lake."

"The lake, huh?"

"Yup. The lake."

Dick grinned and Johnny Vic thought of the Cheshire Cat. It was a bit unnerving. He gulped.

Dick continued, "The lake and . . . ?"

"And?"

"I saw you leave with a backpack. I saw you return without it."

"Oh, that! Well, I . . . well, you see–Uncle Ben and I are going to go on that boat trip and I thought I should have my stuff ready to go. So, I took it outside. Early. So I wouldn't hold Uncle Ben up. You know." Johnny Vic held both hands behind his back, each with fingers crossed. *After all, it's just a little fib,* he thought with a guilty shiver.

"Well, I guess that's one logical explanation," Dick said, although the boy looked very guilty. *Like the proverbial cat that swallowed the canary. It's a logical explanation,* he thought, *but somehow I think there's more to it than that. I guess I'll have to keep my eye on this little guy.*

Dick decided not to push the matter. *At least not yet.* Instead, he changed the subject.

"So, Johnny Vic, are you hungry? I'm thinking about breakfast, myself."

"Yessir!" the boy exclaimed with obvious relief. He was glad that Dick had changed the subject.

"Why don't we go crack a few eggs and surprise the rest of the lazy lugs who are still in bed with the tantalizing

15

smell of bacon?"

"Sounds like a plan. A really good plan!"

***

Chapter 6

Caught again–almost!

The only person who paid attention to the rusty metallic thing on the beach was Johnny Vic. Dick and Linda were talking with Bill and Sue, while Ben and Eric were busy at the grill. *It looks like some kind of hinge,* Johnny Vic thought. Suddenly his eyes widened. *I wonder if it's from one of those old schooners? It sure doesn't look like any hinge I've ever seen before!* He decided to wash it off for a better look, and scurried down to the water. He was busy scrubbing his find when he heard Dick's mellow voice just inches away from him. *Gee,* he thought. *I'm not surprised he was a guard. I bet he was good at sneaking up on thieves.* His cheeks burned. He suddenly felt like a sneaky thief himself. He craned his neck and said, "Oh, Hi, Dick."

"Hi, Johnny Vic. What have you got?"

"Oh, it's just an old metal thing I found on the beach. Nothing special. I think it's a hinge."

"A hinge? Can I see it?"

"Umh, sure."

Johnny Vic grabbed a nearby towel and wiped the water and sand from the hinge, but he did not have to relinquish it after all. Linda had suddenly appeared, catching

17

Dick by the hand, tugging at him with her usual boisterous enthusiasm.

"Dick! Come and see what Bill has–it's his writeup about Lake Champlain!" Her eyes sparkled.

"Sure thing, Dear."

Dick glanced at Johnny Vic with a suspicious glint in his eyes before retreating with his wife; and once again, the boy thought about the Cheshire Cat as he offered his own guilty grin.

Johnny Vic spent the rest of the afternoon trying to act natural. And Dick knew it. *That boy is up to something,* he thought. *And I'm going to keep an eye on him!* His vigilance was rewarded several hours later when he saw the boy head back toward the lake. *Good,* he thought. *Now I can be really sneaky without explaining myself!* He slipped out the door and scurried down the path, right into the middle of a puzzling beam of light. *What's going on? It's like colorful lightning! Oh no . . . I'm falling. Or am I flying? Oh, gosh! Is Johnny Vic caught in this too?*

***

Chapter 7

Back to the . . . *WHEN?##!*

---

*W*ow! Johnny Vic thought. *I made it! I'm back in time again, but I wonder when? And where? And who am I going to meet this time?* He was still wondering about his current exciting circumstance when he heard a groan from the nearby bushes. He dropped to his knees and peered in the direction of the sound.

"Oh no–it's Dick!"

Johnny Vic thought, *Here we go again! I can't seem to go on these adventures alone no matter how careful I am.* He scurried toward the groaning man.

"Are you okay, Dick?"

"I think so. I'm still all in one piece. Nothing seems to be broken." He looked up at the boy. "So what happened? One minute I'm watching you as you turn on that machine–the next minute the world explodes and I'm spinning and falling through a tunnel–with colors swirling all around me."

Dick's puzzlement surrendered to a sudden spurt of fear. "Oh good grief, was it an explosion?" He twirled about to inspect his surroundings. "How big was it? Was anybody hurt? Oh, no, where's Linda?"

Dick whirled around again. "And where's the cabin?

19

Where's the dock?" Then he spun toward Johnny Vic and croaked, "Where the heck are we?"

"Well, if I'm correct, we're in the 1800's. That's if I'm correct."

"The 1800's, like the century? Are you daffy?" Dick grabbed the boy by the shoulders and searched his head for a sign of injury. He was desperately scruffing Johnny Vic's hair when he pulled away.

"I'm fine, Dick. I . . . well, we just traveled back in time is all. It's my metal detector. It's kind of special that way."

"Kind of special? You're telling me we've gone back in time and the thing that did it is, 'kind of special?'"

"Yup."

"Oh, boy." Dick did not even look for anything to sit on. He just plopped to the ground.

"Tell me what really just happened, Johnny Vic. Tell me what really happened."

"I told you. We've gone back in time. I'm not sure how far back, but I think it's probably the 1800's, because I was scanning that hinge. Remember the one I found on the beach? Well, I think it was actually from one of those schooners from the 1800's. I saw one like it at the museum."

As if it would help the situation, he explained, "I think it washed up from the lake during the storm last night."

"Oh, well, of course. That explains it. A hinge washed up in a storm and now we've been propelled back to, umh, what? To the time when it was a baby hinge?" He glared at the boy, who whispered, "I think so. I think that's what happened."

"So, okay. It brought us back in time. So, now, why don't you turn it on and have it bring us back home." His eyebrows shot up. "Now, please?"

"Well, my metal detector will bring us home, eventually, only . . ."

Johnny Vic hesitated because something happened on this trip that he had not experienced before. Two images had appeared on the screen. The first was the hinge, but the second image looked like a button.

Dick pressed, "Only what?"

When the boy continued to hesitate, Dick said, "Don't' be afraid, Johnny Vic. Just tell me what you're thinking. We're in this together, and after all, we both seem to be okay. And I promise I'm not angry. I just want some answers."

"Well, there were two things on the screen. My metal detector picked up two images and I don't know which one sent us here. One was the hinge. I think the other was a button. A metal button."

"A metal button? They've made metal buttons for centuries–tons of centuries!" Dick had a frightening vision of Shakespeare's London and the black plague.

"Who knows where we are," he said. "Or when? We could even be in the middle of the black plague!"

"Well, I don't think you have to worry about that, Dick. It seems to just keep us in the same place, and I think the black plague was in England, wasn't it? I don't remember any mention of it being here." He brightened. "Heck, Dick, Columbus hadn't even discovered America yet!"

Dick ignored the question. He had a more important one of his own. He croaked, "Same place–different century? You're sure?"

"Yes. So far that's it. Same place. Different time– every time."

Johnny Vic plopped down next to Dick. "I met Horace Greeley near Linda's house. And I almost met George Washington at the site of the Old Fort House Museum in Fort Edward, New York. Linda, was there on that one, too!"

Dick thought, *George Washington? Linda has had a recurring dream about meeting him.* He turned toward Johnny Vic with wide-eyed wonder.

They both gulped.

***

21

Chapter 8

Two for the road

The two time travelers decided to do a thorough search of their surroundings. Johnny Vic looked for clues to help determine what century they were in. Dick prayed for clues of an explosion. Despite the similarities between Johnny Vic's story and Linda's dream, he still was not convinced that they had traveled back through time. *After all,* he thought. *It's impossible! It simply cannot happen. But, then again, things sure look different, and yet very much the same. But after all, a blast couldn't have created this much change without leaving some kind of charring or shrapnel!*

In every direction, Dick saw the same countryside–the same mountain peaks, the same shoreline–but there were no houses, no docks, no fields or power lines; *and,* he thought, *I haven't seen a single airplane in the sky either. Usually there's three or four by now.*

Dick said, "I have to admit, Johnny Vic, I'm stymied. So, you say you've been to the 1800's before. So that means you've got experience here. There. I mean, if that's . . . umh . . . where or when we . . . we are."

"Yes."

"And the second trip was to the 1700's, I presume?"

"Yup. And we almost met George Washington. He was on his horse, on his way to visit his medical officer, Dr. Cochran, but the timer was running out and I had to grab Linda so we wouldn't miss our way back home."

Dick was stunned. He did not know which piece of information was more astonishing–the piece about Linda, or about the timer. *Not to mention George Washington,* he thought. The flustered man fired a round of questions.

"Linda? Linda went with you? Why hasn't she ever said anything? And what's this about a timer? Why didn't you tell me we have a timer?"

"Umh, I guess I forgot. These trips make things kind of fuzzy for awhile, you know."

"Well, at least I can believe that. I still feel a bit fuzzy myself." He exhaled noisily and asked, "So where is this timer?"

"It's in the cap that comes with the machine, but," Johnny Vic gulped, "I'm not sure where it is right now. It fell off my head."

He stepped back, expecting a reaction. He needn't have worried. Dick finally was one step ahead of him.

"You haven't lost your cap, Johnny Vic! I saw you rip it off your head and stuff in your bag!" But then his eyes widened. "So, where's your bag?"

Johnny Vic was already racing toward the top of the hill. "It's up here! And I filled it with lots of stuff! Food! And tools! And we can take a look and see how much time we have left! Sometimes you can see what year you're in, too."

Johnny Vic snatched up his backpack. "Okay, the timer's under this flap." His slim fingers carefully unzipped the Velcro to reveal a tiny computer screen. "See? Here it is!" He peered at it. "Holy smokes!"

"What?"

"It says it's 1776!"

"1776?"

"But that's not all. The counter says we've got about thirty-four hours to explore before it brings us someplace else."

"Thirty-four hours? Linda will be crazed with anxiety by then! She'll wonder where I am! And Ben will wonder where you are! And they'll all wonder if I've kidnapped you or something!"

"Relax, Dick! They won't have time to worry! I don't know how it works, exactly, but when we're back in time, several days can pass and yet it's only a couple of hours back home in our own time. They won't have time to miss us."

"Well, I guess you would know." But, Dick's peace of mind was short lived. He croaked, "You just said something about another trip? Does that mean we're not going home from here?"

"Well, it's kind of blinking and there seems to be another date on the screen. It's 1847, so I guess we might get sucked into the 1800's before we go home."

Dick winced, but Johnny Vic brightened. "But there's only a few hours in that century!"

***

Chapter 9

The gold!

Dick and Johnny Vic decided to travel south along the shore of the lake. Since they would be spending three days in this pristine new environment, they wanted to find a safe place to stay. It would have to be a spot where no one could sneak up on them.

"After all," Dick said, "the native tribes were not always friendly. Poor Father Joques and other missionaries who traveled this area were murdered, you know."

"Yes, I know. But I did learn some Iroquois from an Iroquois boy in the 1700's! I think I'll be able to tell them we're friendly."

"Well, that's great, Johnny Vic. But, I think I read somewhere that different tribes had different dialects. Of course, I could be wrong–I'm certainly no expert on the matter."

"Gee, I never thought about that. I don't know if it's true or not, Dick."

SEVERAL MINUTES LATER, Dick grabbed Johnny Vic by the arm. "Shhhhhh! I think I hear someone! Sounds like they're coming this way!"

They darted behind a mound of earth and rocks and watched as a solitary man approached. The stranger was wearing a long brown robe and Johnny Vic could see a tiny black cap on the top of his head.

"Is that one of those Jesuit priests?" he asked.

Dick's eyes were bulging. He thought, "It's true! My gosh, it's true! He does look like a Jesuit priest from centuries ago!" Instinctively, he reached toward the boy.

"No! Don't show yourself yet. Let's wait a few minutes and see what he's doing."

"Okay," Johnny Vic whispered.

THE MAN STOPPED to survey his surroundings. He had been pulling a small cart that appeared to be very heavy. Johnny's imagination filled in the blanks. *Jesuit gold! I bet that cart's full of gold! The gold they were supposed to have hidden!*

The man strode toward a rocky overhang. He spent several minutes lifting rocks and rolling boulders. He was obviously creating a shelter of some sort. *Or a place to hide the gold,* Johnny Vic thought.

Moments later the boy knew he was right. The man in the long brown robe removed several heavy gold bars from the bags in his cart and placed them in the cavern that he had created. Johnny Vic counted sixteen gold bars.

Dick was bug eyed.

They were almost ready to approach the man when, as Dick would later say, "The woods exploded with angry red men!"

The scary intruders advanced toward the robed man with murderous clubs raised high.

Dick snatched up his young companion and pulled him backwards, out of sight. As he did so, he fought a heart-wrenching wave of guilt. *I can't let it get to me,* he thought. *I have to keep Johnny Vic safe.*

As if he could read the man's mind, Johnny Vic whispered, "We can't help him yet, Dick. There are too many of them. And besides, I'm not sure we're supposed to change things too much–you know what I mean?"

"Yes, Johnny. Of course, you're right. Say, how did you get to be such a clever young man?"

"I've had a lot of good teachers."

With a wistful smile, Johnny Vic thought about the wise old Iroquois woman who had taught him so much on his last adventure. And then he realized, *Gee, Sweet Eyes of the Morning and her grandson Lightfoot are probably just a hundred miles away or so! Wouldn't it be great if . . .* a scuffle below brought his attention back to his current adventure.

*** *

Chapter 10

Dreams can feel so real!

Linda was dreaming. It was that recurring dream that had begun shortly after her visit to Fort Edward, New York. She had gone to the Old Fort House Museum, also known as the Smyth House, with Johnny Vic and Ben. In the dream, she saw George Washington–was actually about to meet him–and then she'd be swallowed up into a kaleidoscopic tunnel.

And Johnny Vic would be spinning and falling with her in this stunning vortex of color and light.

And then she would wake up.

"Oh! It's that dream again!"

Linda sat up and shook her head. The dream was so vivid she could even remember the sparkle in the eyes of the horse that George Washington was riding. *It was as if he knew he was carrying a great man,* she thought. *And Washington himself–he seemed so real! I feel as if I actually did see him!*

Linda wondered for a moment if there were some significant psychological reason why she never actually met the great man in this dream. She was still pondering the question when Bill and Sue Clark caught her attention.

"So, that must have been quite a dream," Sue said.

"You were flailing your arms like crazy–was it one of those dreams about falling?"

"You could say that. But . . . oh, Sue! It was frightening and wonderful all at once! And so vivid. I've had this dream several times over the past year and it's always the same–George Washington is approaching on horseback and I get sucked away by this colorful vortex before I actually meet him."

"George Washington, you say? Wouldn't I have a few questions for that man."

"I bet you would, Bill," Sue chuckled.

Bill ignored her taunt. "I'd like to hear his opinion of these nutcases who are insisting that we take God out of our schools and public buildings, for one. After all–did you know that he actually said, in his farewell address to the nation, that he believed that religion and morality needed to be in politics? I can't for the life of me, Linda, understand how anybody can say he–or any of the other founding fathers for that matter–wanted God out of our government. After all, most of them were clergymen or associated with Christianity one way or another. And that's another sore spot, if you ask me. Why on earth they say there was only a handful of them is beyond me. There were over a 150 founding fathers who signed the first few important documents in our nation's history!"

Bill slapped at the air with one finger and chuckled, "And maybe I'd ask the first George W if he really did chop down that cherry tree."

"SO LINDA, ARE YOU going to stick around for awhile? Maybe see the newest displays at that Maritime Museum?"

"Of course. I'm sure it's going to be wonderful!" She jumped to her feet and looked around. Her eyes traveled from north to south and she reveled in the beauty of Lake Champlain.

"It's so exciting to have been asked to join the committee! I have lots of ideas for celebrating the 400th anniversary of this lake. And some of them include fund raising to help fight the pollution!"

"You getting involved in that, too? That's one of the reasons Sue and I are here. Killing two birds with one stone, and so forth."

Sue said, "Linda, I bet you have a lot of good ideas. I know I can't wait to get started."

"By the way," Linda asked with a slight tremer in her voice. "Have you seen Dick lately?"

***

Chapter 11

Spiders and Stakes!

$\mathbf{A}$ nasty black spider was crawling toward Isaiah's face. His eyes widened with disgust and a little bit of fear, but he did not reach out to brush it away–he couldn't. Isaiah duPaul St. Romaine could not move at all! His wrists and ankles were tightly bound with rawhide to stakes that had been pounded securely into the ground. His body had been stretched as far as it could be stretched.

Isaiah watched with morbid fascination as the eight-legged creature scuttled toward him. It would stop momentarily, then it would come closer. *Probably checking its surroundings,* he thought. *Ghastly thing probably senses my body heat and she's checking me out. Well, she won't be able to drag me to her web–not unless she can untie these knots!* Isaiah tried to laugh at the thought, but the only sound he could make was a dry, coughing gurgle.

He turned his head away in dispair. The spider was the least of his troubles right now. The pain from the beating he took was unbearable enough, but, his bindings had been soaked in water and eventually they would shrink. The pressure would cut off his circulation and might even stretch him more.

"Oh God–why did this happen? Must I die this way? Is this to be the end of my life?"

Isaiah's spasms and impassioned cry startled the black spider and it scurried toward a nearby log. "Well, thank you for that, my Lord," he sighed. "Thank you for sending that wretched creature away."

BECAUSE HE WAS a devout Christian, Isaiah's thoughts traveled to his teachings and eventually to the Lord himself. To the cross. To the unrelenting mockery and suffering that Jesus Christ must have experienced when he was on the cross. *At least I am resting on the ground,* he thought. *Without nails in my wrists and feet.*

ISAIAH's cry woke Johnny Vic up. He and Dick had been dozing beneath the protective branches of a pine tree that formed a canopy-like cover. Last night, after they witnessed the capture of the robed man, Dick had whispered that deer often slept beneath branches like this.

Dick was also awake. He stretched stiff arms and wriggled his toes and whispered to his young companion. "Did you hear that, Johnny?"

"I sure did. It sounded like the guy was crying out or something."

"Yes, so he's still alive, thank God. I think I'll check it out. But you . . ." he said with a croaking whisper, " . . . you should stay put. There's no sense in both of us sticking our necks out."

"But what if the Indians see you?"

"I'll be careful. You know we can't hide here forever. Besides, we left your backpack up on the hill and we need that timer!"

The pine branches were so low, Dick could not sit up. He had to roll himself out of their protective embrace. Two stars were still visible in the misty morning sky. He wondered which stars they were. He wondered if he would be able to recognize them if he and Johnny Vic returned to their friends and families. *No!* He corrected himself. *Not 'if' we return home–it's WHEN we return. I'm going to look for those same two stars WHEN we get home."*

LIKE ISAIAH'S SPIDER, Dick scuttled up the hill, then stopped. Scuttled again, and stopped again. Each time, he was listening and watching, feeling and waiting, ready to escape from even the slightest hint of danger. Apparently there was none. He reached the backpack unharmed. *So far, so good,* he thought. *Well, I guess I should take a peek at the other side of this hill. I hope it isn't too gruesome!*

Dick crawled to the top and gazed at the panoramic scene before him. Lake Champlain was absolutely beautiful. The moon spilled its rays across the mirror-like surface. A fish jumped and somehow the soft splash felt reassuring. Dick forced his vision back toward the water's edge and then inland, into the grassy area where the Mohawks had tied the unfortunate robed man to stakes in the ground.

"Oh–they really did torture people like that! They really did leave them to die!" He cringed, suddenly aware of the sound of his own voice. *Good Lord,* he thought. *Did they leave any of their members behind to watch their handiwork? If so, did they hear me?* Dick sucked in a gallon of air. He froze. Only his eyes moved as he surveyed his surroundings, once again poised for flight. Only seconds passed, but he was already thinking, *Why does time seem to stand still when you're afraid?*

He did finally decide that none of the Indians had been left behind, but he still crawled quietly and carefully back to Johnny Vic who had dutifully remained beneath their tree.

"Johnny!" he whispered. "That poor man is still down there. They stretched him out and tied him up."

Dick pushed the backpack toward Johnny Vic and said, "Here, take this. I'm going to see if there's anything I can do for him, but I want you to stay here until I call for you. For goodness sake, don't leave this spot until I call for you."

"But Dick . . ."

"No buts, Johnny Vic. None! And if I don't come back for you or call to you–or if you hear anything that sounds suspicious–you're to stay right here and wait for that timer to ring, or buzz, or do whatever it does, to bring you back home."

"Awe, come on, Dick. It's my fault you're here. I can't leave you–I won't!"

Dick's voice softened. "Now listen–I was a guard for a lot of years. I've had a lot of training. If anyone can stay safe out there, it's me." He stared into Johnny Vic's eyes. "Believe me?"

"Yes. I guess I do."

"Good. And the last thing I need right now is to be worrying about you–I need all my attention to be on my surroundings. Got it?"

"Yup. Okay. I'll stay put. But be careful, Dick! Please, be careful!"

"I will."

JOHNNY VIC WAITED. It felt like an hour had passed, but he knew it was only a matter of minutes. *Jeepers,* he thought. *Dick's been gone a long time. I wonder how much longer I should wait? Jeepers, I wish I had a watch.* He stared at his wrist and then he grinned. It was a big, huge grin. An, 'I-know-what-I-can-do-after-all' kind of grin.

I'll count to 500. I'll count, and if he's not back by then, I'll sneak up the hill for a peek.

Johnny Vic rolled over and tucked his pack under his head. It was lumpy, but he did not care. He was worried about Dick. He was also thinking about the gold bars that he'd seen last night. *Real gold! Real treasure!* He stretched his legs and started to count. Several minutes passed before he came to the end of his counting.

"Four hundred and ninety seven," he whispered. "Four hundred and ninety eight." It felt as if he had been counting forever. "Four hundred and ninety ni-----ne . . ."

In a strange effort to be fair, Johnny Vic stretched out the number as long as his breath held out. Then he gasped,

"Five hundred!"

He immediately rolled off his backpack and listened for trouble. Birds were chirping and a mosquito was buzzing around, but that is all that Johnny Vic could hear. *Okay,* he thought. *I think I've waited long enough. I've gotta see if Dick is okay.*

***

Chapter 12

Are you an angel?

Isaiah heard footsteps. *My Lord,* he thought. *Please have mercy on this wretched body and upon my soul. If it is the savages that approach, let death come quickly.* With his arms bound, Isaiah could not make the sign of the cross. He whispered, "I'm sure you'll undertand, Lord, that I would if I could."

The footsteps were almost upon him and he braced himself for more pain, but when they stopped just inches from his head, nothing happened. He only heard the labored breathing of one person.

"May my Lord Jesus Christ have mercy on me," he uttered softly. "May you have mercy on my wretched soul."

DICK DROPPED TO his knees.

"It's okay, Sir. I'm here to help you. I'm here to help." Dick made a mental note to thank Johnny Vic for packing so many useful items in his backpack. He said, "I'm going to cut these leather bindings."

Carefully, he grasped the strap that held Isaiah's left arm and sawed at it with a knife.

"What?" Isaiah murmured as he blinked at the

stranger with the soft voice. "You are setting me free? Are you an angel from my Lord?"

When the crusty strip of leather surrendered to the serrated blade, Isaiah's arm flopped painfully to the ground. Dick scooted closer and severed the other strap with one swift cut. The man closed his eyes and moaned, and then he said, "Thank you."

"It's okay, don't try to talk yet."

Dick quickly cut the bindings from Isaiah's legs and then set to work, gently rubbing his arms. "I think we need to get the circulation back," he said. "It'll take a few minutes, but I'm sure you'll be okay."

Isaiah surrendered himself to the gentle man's care. It felt so good to experience the touch of human kindness. *Soooo goooood!*

***

Chapter 13

So, we're in the 1700's?

"Who are you?" Johnny Vic asked. He was offering the dazed man a nutty protein bar. "Are you a Jesuit priest?"

"No, my child. I am not a priest. I wear this robe because the natives usually respect those who wear it. Unfortunately, those savages who tied me up were acting at the behest of Nathaniel Quatrain." Isaiah chopped at the air angrily and explained, "Nathaniel is a very bad man."

Dick asked, "So why would a man like that want to hurt you?"

"It is because I know his secret. I know that he is a traitor to our King."

"Did he steal that gold, then?"

"Gold? What do you know of the gold?"

"We saw you hide it."

"You must not touch it! You must not!"

"Don't worry–we won't! We won't!"

"Gold!" Isaiah spat the word. "It causes so much pain. So much deceit."

"So, will you tell us your story? I assume you've taken it back from Nathaniel?"

"Yes. I did. And yes, I will tell you about it, but there

is not much to tell. I was traveling with Father Isaac Frances St. Thornbraun. Nathaniel was acting as our guide. On order of our King, Father Isaac was bringing the word of our Lord to the natives of this land. He also was carrying a small fortune in gold that he said would be useful when the time came to build churches and schools."

Isaiah shook his head. "I tried to tell him it was dangerous–carrying that much gold. That it would be temptation itself. And of course, Nathaniel fell under the lure of that temptation. I recognized one of the savages that attacked me. I am certain that he is one I had seen with Nathaniel."

"So, why did they just leave you? Why didn't they try to take the gold?"

"Oh, I do not think that Nathaniel told them about it. I am sure he would have promised them some trinkets if they produced proof that they had stopped me." A growling sound emerged from his throat. He said, "And they did take my cross."

Dick and Johnny Vic watched as Isaiah reached toward his throat, his fingers settling upon the place where the cross undoubtedly had hung. "I am sure he will be coming for the gold himself. He would not want to share it with anyone."

Dick's eyes flew open. "It sounds like we need to get out of here, then! He could be on his way right now!"

"Do not worry. He is quite far from here. It will take several days just for the savages to reach him and show him my cross."

Dick thought, *Thank God this is the age before the automobile.* He nodded toward Isaiah and said, "Good. So, now what do you want to do?"

"I must continue northward, toward an agreed upon rendezvous. Admiral Bain will eventually come to take me home."

"And the gold?"

"We will sail back here to pick it up. It is too dangerous to travel with it, and I would not want to endanger the Ferris family with it."

Johnny Vic exclaimed, "The Ferris family? Do you mean Peter Ferris and his son, Squire? Wow! By the way, what year is this?"

Isaiah blinked. "Why, it is 1776, the year of our Lord Christ, of course."

Johnny whispered to Dick, "It's the year Benedict Arnold stopped the British at the Battle of Valcour!" He did not dare to remind Dick that the battle took place in October, on this very date.

Johnny Vic looked at Isaiah with renewed interest. "So, could we come with you?"

"Of course. Peter Ferris is a man of faith. And his homestead is not far from here."

And today's the day! Johnny Vic thought. *Wow, I may not get to see Samuel de Champlain, but who cares? I'm going to see Benedict Arnold's greatest battle–the Battle of Valcour! I just know it!*

"Let's go!" Johnny Vic exclaimed as he scrambled up the path with renewed vigor.

DICK HAD SEEN the gleam in his young friend's eyes. He thought, *Ohhh noooo. What's the little Dickens up to now?*

***

Chapter 14

Benedict Arnold Remembers

Benedict Arnold clutched his commission papers in a joyful waggle before stashing them safely away in the captain's quarters of his new ship. His eyes sparkled with excitement; his people had just built 15 war ships and they were about to embark on an important mission. It would be the very first battle of the United States Navy. Congress had issued the orders to build, ". . . with all expedition, as many gallies and armed vessels as . . . shall be sufficient to make us indisputably masters of the lakes–Champlain and George."

And now, Benedict Arnold was finally in command of those ships. He closed his eyes and thought about his years of struggle to be recognized as a leader in battle. Just 17 months ago, on May 10, 1775, to be precise, he and Ethan Allen's bunch had joined together to capture Fort Ticonderoga. And what an amazing victory it was! Benedict paused at the threshold of his quarters, his mind suddenly flooded with memories. He grinned and shook his head at the thought of the energetic Green Mountain Boys. *I must confess,* he thought wryly, *that those ruffians from Vermont fought well. However, the sluggish Brits were no match for any of us–that is for sure–but we can thank our Lord for that!* Benedict Arnold gave praise to God for each victory and accomplishment that he had experienced during his career as a military man.

Colonel Arnold held his grin as he closed the door behind him. He reached for the ladder that would lead him up to the main deck. He began to climb the rungs, then stopped to listen to the activity above.

There was the high-pitched squeal of metal against metal when a gust of wind hit the main sail and the sudden *thwack* from the line being extended as a sailor sheeted in the jib. There was the soft slosh of wet rag against wooden floorboard as another man swabbed the deck. And above all of these sounds that Benedict Arnold loved so much, seagulls squawked greedily as they fought for their share of food. *Our feathered followers squabble as much as we humans,* Benedict decided as his eyes drank in the extraordinary views from aboard the ship that he did not realize was destined for the most important battle that occurred on Lake Champlain.

For a moment he paused and wondered if the lake's namesake, Samuel de Champlain, had felt thusly buoyed as he sailed these very waters. Benedict Arnold loved every sound and sight aboard ship–but even more, he loved the feel of victory when it coursed through his veins. *Victory in the name of freedom,* he thought. *Freedom and victory–two of the most pleasant and lovely words that can befall the ears of my fellow countrymen.*

With a swift nod of his head, he thought, *General Washington should certainly be pleased with our victories. I know that he appreciated the artillery that we were able to extract from Fort Ticonderoga!*

We have surely made a difference for our cause, he thought. *We surprised the Brits at Ticonderoga last year without a single fire of a gun. And our people had taken control of Fort Crown Point and Skenesborough, as well. And, with this pretty lady and her fellow ships, we'll stop the British advance once and for all.*

Colonel Arnold strode toward the helm in search of his second mate. He wanted to confirm that they would reach Ferris Bay on schedule.

***

Chapter 15

Come to my web . . .

Through squinty eyes, Benedict Arnold peered up the lake. He was waiting for the first enemy flagship to come into view. *It won't be long now,* he thought. And as he waited, his mind ran through dozens of scenes from previous battles. *The fire. The screams. The relentless noise of cannon blasts.*

He cupped his eyes with his hands for a moment and forced himself to focus upon this day's enemy. A series of words flitted across his mind as he thought about the British invaders and their ships. *Graceful. Deadly. Arrogant. Strong.* He glanced at his own ships and crew and remembered what had been said about them. They had been called 'a rag-a-tag crew. Inept.'

Benedict Arnold spat upon the deck. *Inept? I think not! My men are anything but that. They are strong. And they are with God's grace. Oh, yes, we may be a makeshift crew, but we're determined. And brave. Brave to the very last man.*

Benedict Arnold aimed his eyes back toward the north. *Come you vile creatures. Come into my web that has been spun by valiant men. We are waiting for you. Come!*

***

Chapter 16

The sample

Ben studied the vials of water that Eric had taken from Lake Champlain.

"So, what's the verdict, Eric . . . any improvement?"

"Too soon to tell. You can't go by the look of it. But, then again, we have seen a little bit of improvement over the past year or two."

"How 'little'?"

"Well, it's measurable."

"Doesn't sound like much, but it's a start."

"Yeah. It's a start. And maybe these samples will bring us some good news."

"I'd love to be able to add some positive news about your efforts to my story."

"I'd love it, too, Ben. So, I tell you what–I'll get the info to you asap. Right now, I'm taking the samples in the little test tubes back to the chemists at our laboratory. They'll add chemicals that turn blue when they react with the phosphorous."

"Turns it blue, huh?"

"Yup. As blue as the sky. And then they'll use a special instrument called a spectrophotometer to measure just how blue the sample is. That tells them how much phosphorous was in the water."

"And what about those bottles over there?" Ben pointed toward a set of bottles that were still in the basket.

"Well, those larger bottles are going to be analyzed for dissolved oxygen. We want to make sure there's enough oxygen in the lake for the fish to live."

ERIC PLACED THE last sample into his carrier and snapped the lid shut. "Okay. Let's head back to the lab and see what we can see–Jabber Lee."

Ben did a double take and Eric said, "Good grief, I've been hanging around you and Johnny Vic a little too much."

***

Chapter 17

God's Grace

Isaiah looked at his feet and said softly, "It is not easy to follow God's word, whether you are a priest or not. But missionaries go to dangerous places because we wish to spread the Word and bring new Christians to the fold. I help do this because I believe we must save their souls.

"But as I said, I am not a Jesuit. I am not a priest. I am simply a believer. A believer of the Gospel of Jesus Christ." With those words, Isaiah's eyes lit up. "I have read the Bible. I have read His words. I believe in His message of grace. His message of faith. And I feel certain that we each must have a personal relationship with Him." Isaiah reached out and touched Johnny Vic's shoulder. "You," he said. "You, even a young boy like you, should speak to God. Pray to Him. And most of all, develop a relationship with Him. This is–I believe–what He wants. The priests, they want to speak to Him for you. And perhaps that is good. But, they should not stop you from developing a personal relationship with our Lord. And, most of all, I believe it is of the utmost importance for us to share His word and give others that opportunity!"

WHEN ISAIAH was strong enough to walk, Dick and Johnny Vic accompanied him along the shore. They stopped occasionally to rest and refresh themselves.

"Look at the water, Dick. It's so clear!"

"I noticed."

**

Chapter 18

Almost there

Isaiah had gained his strength back quickly. He was remarkably strong and Johnny Vic thought they had walked forever, when they stopped for a final rest. Isaiah said the Ferris homestead was less than an hour's walk away. They were being very careful to avoid being seen, but Johnny Vic could not help himself–every now and then he would race ahead of the two men and stop to peer at the lake. He was actually hoping to get a glimpse of the American ships–a glimpse of Benedict Arnold's makeshift navy.

Johnny Vic knew that the amazing Battle of Valcour would soon be fought. He took a deep breath, filling his lungs with the uplifting essence of crisp country air and seized the moment to study his surroundings. He wanted to imprint the very essence of this day within his memory. He peered up at the clouds and noticed each shape. They were so much like the clouds that he had seen on the dock with his uncle. *Gee,* he thought. *Some things never change. The clouds here today look pretty much the same, but I guess somehow they do seem a little brighter.* He looked down toward his feet and recognized the pillowy tufts of reindeer moss. He looked toward the west and heard the familiar calls of chickadees and crows. It was all so familiar, and yet so different. *It's fresher,* he thought. *Fresh, like it was just born.*

A moment of sadness threatened to overtake Johnny Vic. He felt that the world had grown weary in the centuries that led to his time. *Weary and polluted,* he thought sadly. *Weary and polluted.* But, Johnny Vic was never one to let sadness stop him. He believed that some day people would get it right. He also believed that he was given this unbelievable chance to see his world when it was fresh so that he could make a difference in his own lifetime. But, he just had to see that battle, if even only for a moment! To see it with his own eyes! To read about it in his history books, and to actually remember it, too! *In full color!*

Johnny Vic could just imagine himself, back in his own time, reading a textbook description of the Battle of Valcour. It would probably say, 'It was October 14, 1776.' *Yes,* he thought. *That's what it'll say, but the next time I read about it, I'll remember that there were clouds floating in the bright blue sky that day. And I'll remember the birds, and the fish splashing in the lake, and the leaves crunching beneath my feet. I'll remember it all!*

The text would also probably say, 'Benedict Arnold and his men put up a valiant fight, but they were defeated. They fled in the dark of night, their oars bound with rags to muffle the splashes as they slipped silently past their enemy. However, their brave efforts were not a total failure. They had crippled the great British navy. Crippled them enough to force them to retreat back to the Canadian border. And in doing so, they had given their countrymen the gift of time.

JOHNNY VIC SIGHED with pleasure. He was going to write a wonderful report for his teacher!

***

Chapter 19

Where's Dick?

Linda felt a little uneasy. Her husband had vanished without a word. *It's not like him,* she thought. *But, then again, he did say something about Johnny Vic. He's probably with the boy right now. I'm sure there's nothing to worry about.*

To take her mind off her concerns, Linda decided to read Bill Clark's essay on Lake Champlain. She had always appreciated the importance of the lake's role in history. But, she was equally intrigued by Bill's claim that it had been recognized as the sixth great lake on March 6, 1998, with Senate Bill number 927. She wanted to learn more about that story–especially since Congress had rescinded the proclamation because of the demands of certain politicians from other parts of the country–politicians who did not want any federal money going toward the Lake Champlain region.

"Well! I think we should fight that decision!" she exclaimed.

With that thought in mind, Linda decided to find a quiet spot outside where she could read. She strode toward her car to get Bill's essay and to get her radio. She wanted to keep an ear out for the local weather forecast. *Especially*

with that hurricane that's heading toward the East Coast!
No one here has even mentioned it.

***

Chapter 20

Run, Johnny Vic . . . run!

Dick tapped Johnny Vic on the shoulder and whispered, "Hey, have you checked your timer lately? How much time do we have left?"

"Umh," Johnny Vic grunted as he checked to make sure their new friend was out of earshot. "Let me see, there's, umh, three hours left."

"Okay. Three hours. I can deal with that."

Dick gave Johnny Vic a sly salute and slowed his pace. He thought he'd pick the brain of this stranger who had lived hundreds of years before him.

"So, Isaiah, what was it like–traveling across the ocean with your captain?"

Isaiah grimaced and said, "It was smelly. And some days it was hot. I could not breath. And the waves! We would go up and down. Up and down. I felt very sick. Many times."

"I'm sorry to hear that,"

To himself Dick muttered, *I can't believe I'm having a normal conversation with a man from the 1700's and I'm expecting to be traveling through time in three hours, or so. I simply can't believe it!* He pinched himself.

"Ouch!" *Oh fudge,* he thought. *I guess I'm awake after all.*

Isaiah looked at Dick. "What is wrong?"

"Wrong? Nothing. I mean, I, umh, stubbed my toe. Yes, I stubbed my toe, but it's nothing."

DICK BEGAN TO FEEL like a yo-yo as he quickened his pace once again. He had another question for the boy.

"Say, Johnny Vic," he whispered. "Do we need to stick together to be transported?"

"I think so. I mean, you're only the second person to travel back with me, and I guess it's because you were pretty close."

"You . . . think . . . so. Umh, that does not sound very reassuring."

Johnny Vic looked at him and blinked.

"Well, let's hope we don't get separated."

Dick was about to say, "Don't you dare go off somewhere," when fear clutched at his heart and he shouted, "Run, Johnny Vic. Run!"

***

Chapter 21

Oh no! Where's Johnny Vic?

What are we going to do now? Dick was desperate. Two Mohawk braves had grabbed him and another had chased after Johnny Vic who was now nowhere to be seen.

Wow, they're just like the pictures! Except they don't have any war paint on their faces. He thought about that for a moment then realized it was probably a good thing. *Maybe it means they don't consider me to be a prisoner of war. Maybe they're just curious or suspicious. I guess it's also a good sign they haven't strung me up like they strung up Isaiah. But, man! That young one's eyes are scary–he looks crazy!*

Dick was resting against a tree trunk. His captors had motioned for him to sit down; they had not even tied him up. *I guess they don't think I'm much of a threat,* he thought. He wondered how much time had passed since the timer had been at the three-hour mark. *What can I do? I hope Johnny Vic shows up. Oh, no, wait! He can't! It's too dangerous! But, I still don't know what these guys are up to. Good grief, what if we transport them back home with us?*

Dick tried not to think another thought about the matter. He forced his mind to focus on his surroundings. And he suddenly realized that Isaiah was talking to the red men. And he was smiling! *So!* Dick thought hopefully. *They must be friendly after all. Well, good. Maybe they'll help us find Johnny Vic. That would be a good thing.*

Dick soon realized he would get no help from the crazy-eyed natives. Isaiah had just given them some kind of trinket and they vanished as suddenly as they had appeared.

"They will not harm us," Isaiah said. "And now we should go. Luckily your little friend had run in the right direction."

***

Chapter 22

Oh, please! Don't let me sneeze!

Johnny Vic felt like he had been running forever. His lungs burned from the strain. Desperately, he glanced around, his breath still coming in painful, raspy gasps, when he spied a large hollow tree.

"Jeepers, I wonder if that's big enough to hold me?" He fell to his knees and peered inside. It was icky. But, it seemed big enough. He squirmed in as far as he could, then eased into a more comfortable position. Black stuff clung to his sneakers. His hands. His hair. But he did not care. This tiny, slimy space was probably going to be a very safe place to hide. And there was no time to waste.

Johnny Vic knew he had to stay quiet, but it was not easy! His heart pounded so hard you could see it beating in his chest. And it was almost impossible to control his raspy breath. *Oh no! They're here!* Johnny Vic could hear stealthy footsteps, mere inches away. And then, he felt a tickle in his nose! Oh, please, God, no! Don't let me sneeze!

***

Chapter 23

Run, you red devil!

Squire Ferris dropped his sledgehammer and plopped down with a sense of accomplishment. It was only 9:30 in the morning and he had just finished pounding the last fence pole into the ground. He had been working on this new length of fence for three days. It was hard work, but he felt up to the challenge.

"By crackers, I done it! I got those blasted poles all set up just like my Daddy wanted–and it's almost time for the warships that peddler told us about! I can't wait to see them!"

Squire reached for his shirt so he could use it to mop the sweat from his brow. Although the air had been crisp and frosty at sunrise, it had quickly warmed up enough for him to remove his shirt; and although he was only fourteen years old, his strong, tanned muscles rippled with each pound of the hammer. Squire appreciated every ray of warmth that the sun had to offer on this beautiful fall day. He cupped his hand over his eyes and stared toward Ferris Cove. A steady breeze tickled the surface of the water, creating diamond-like sparkles that blinked their way across the bay that bore his family name.

Squire loved this view, but his mind was not on its beauty at the moment–he was waiting for a glimpse of his hero, Benedict Arnold. A friend of the family had recently stopped with a tale about how Colonel Arnold and that ruffian Ethan Allen had captured Fort Ticonderoga from the Brits without firing a single shot.

"And now," the man had said, "they was comin' up from Skenesborough to beat them Brits once and for all!" Jerome had also said Arnold's men, "was workin' hard to get us all free from British rule."

Squire's father said he thought it would be good for commerce. Squire did not know what 'commerce' meant, but he figured if his Daddy was agreeable to it, then it must be a good thing. *And anyway,* he thought, *freedom is such a grand thing to fight for.*

Squire's eyes scanned across the bay once again and then stopped to open wide.

"Oh, no! I left my lunch sack back at the old hollow tree!" He picked up his rifle and sprinted toward the edge of the field.

SQUIRE FERRIS STOPPED beside a paper white birch and v-e-r-y c-a-r-e-f-u-l-l-y pulled his rifle off from his shoulder. The thief that had stolen his Daddy's chickens was standing just a few yards ahead of him–near the old hollow tree. He steadied himself, aimed, and fired at the sleek red fox.

"Ah ha!" he exclaimed. "Go ahead and run, you red devil–but I bet you won't be skulking around here anymore!"

The blast of Squire's gun had startled the fox, forcing it to dart through the ragged brush. But Squire realized that something else was also trampling through the forest. *That sounds a lot bigger than the fox–I wonder if it was a bear?* He stepped closer to get a better look. That's when he heard the shout.

***

Chapter 24

What a sight!

One minute Johnny Vic was desperately fighting a sneeze, the next minute, a gunshot rang through the air and the scary red man was even more desperately racing away from him. *Jeepers,* he thought. *I don't know who fired that shot, but I'm sure glad he did.*

"Hello!" he shouted. "Please don't shoot me!"

Johnny Vic crawled out of the dirty crevice and was busy brushing the icky decay from his jeans when the blonde-haired boy approached.

"Hello." Squire said. "I'm sorry if I scared you. I was not shooting at you–I was aiming at a fox. I think he's been stealing our chickens. By the way, did you see a bear? I seem to have frightened something else and it sounded much larger than a fox."

"It was. I mean, it was bigger than a fox, all right. Actually, it was an Indian who was chasing me. I thought he was going to scalp me or something."

"Goodness. I'm glad I fired my gun, then."

"Boy, I'm glad, too. You probably saved my life." He held out his hand. "By the way, I'm Johnny Vic. What's your name?"

"I'm Squire Ferris."

Johnny Vic's eyes opened wide. *Squire Ferris? Hot dog!*

***

Chapter 25

The Battle of Valcour? Oh no!

Squire Ferris said, "Someone is coming! We must hide, Johnny Vic."

Johnny Vic said, "No, it's okay. That's my friend Dick, and a nice man we met."

"Are you sure?"

"Yes."

"Okay."

Dick shouted, "Johnny! Thank God you're okay! Thank God we've found you!" He sprinted toward the two boys.

WHEN DICK AND ISAIAH approached, Squire held up his hand in welcome.

"Hello. I'm Squire Ferris. I'm truly glad you're not the Queen's men."

Dick introduced himself. "Hello, Squire. I'm Dick and I can assure you, I'm an American."

"Are you here to join Benedict Arnold?"

"Benedict Arnold? You mean the soldier?"

Yes, of course! His ships are due to come here any time now. I cannot wait to see them! They are so brave, don't you think?"

Dick glared at Johnny Vic. *Benedict Arnold? We're going to see Benedict Arnold, here on Lake Champlain, as in the Battle of Valcour? Oh, my Lord. The Battle of Valcour!* As his mind raced through these unsettling thoughts, Dick continued to glare at Johnny Vic who was clearly trying to look innocent.

ISAIAH OFFERED HIS hand. "I am Isaiah duPaul St. Romain and I can assure you that I am not here to participate on either side in this struggle. I am here to do God's work."

"Well, I come from a family of faith and I am sure my father would welcome you to our home." Squire smiled openly and confided, " . . . and my mother is always happy to set more plates upon the table–that is for certain."

"If that is an invitation, I gladly accept."

"Splendid." Squire turned his gaze toward Johnny Vic and Dick. "And you? Will you both come as well?"

"Yes, we would love to meet your family."

"Well then, follow me."

Squire Ferris picked up his tools and said, "We must go this way." He wanted to stay on the hill and watch for the warships, but he was too well mannered to ignore his guests. He knew his mother would love the company. As he trudged back toward his home with his guests in tow, he wondered how he would be able to get away to see Colonel Arnold's ships.

He need not have worried. Johnny Vic had no intention of missing the battle.

***

Chapter 26

Dick is finally believing it

$\mathbf{D}$ick thought, *Now let me see . . .* as he trudged toward the Ferris homestead. *I saw the museum's movie depicting the Battle of Valcour. The struggle started during the day and went on into the night.*

Dick squeezed his eyes shut for just a moment to help focus on what he had learned at the Lake Champlain Maritime Museum.

The Battle of Valcour took place on October 11, 1776. The British ships were sailing past Valcour Island and the Americans were concealed on the lee side; but the wind put the Brits at a disadvantage. They could not bring all of their ships into the battle. Even though the first canon fire had erupted early in the day, darkness fell before the British fleet could claim victory.

As a result of the battle, the Americans lost 11 ships and ten percent of their men. Some of the ships had been sunk by enemy fire, some deliberately destroyed to keep them out of the hands of the British. By nightfall the Americans were desperate, and Colonel Benedict Arnold crafted a miraculous retreat under cover of fog and darkness. With oiled rags wrapped around their paddles, they stealthily rowed past the menacing British warships.

Once the British Commander, Colonel Carleton, re-alized that he had been duped by the crew of the pitiful American Navy, he chased after them for two days. Eventually his men overtook the brash bunch, but not before they beached and burned their ships to keep them out of his hands.

DICK FELT SORRY FOR Benedict Arnold and for all of the men who had lost their lives in that battle on behalf of freedom. And to make matters worse, Benedict Arnold eventually would feel betrayed by his own country and would become one of the most infamous traitors in American history.

And yet, without him, Dick thought, *this great country might not have survived its infancy. Because of their bravery on this day, Benedict Arnold and all of his men had gone down in history as heroes. They had lost the battle, but they had forced the most powerful naval force in the world to turn back and lick its wounds. Arnold and his men had also succeeded in stopping Carleton's attempt to cut the colonies in half.*

Thank you, God. And thank you Benedict Arnold, Dick thought. Because if Carleton had been successful, he would have gained full control of the Champlain Basin and the Hudson River Valley.

Even without a military background, Dick understood that if the British had succeeded in that plot, it would have been disastrous for the Colonists. He also knew that the delay had given the Colonists the time they needed to strengthen their forces. And of equal importance, Benedict Arnold's efforts had won the respect of the French, who formed an alliance with the cagey Colonists. They offered the strength of their own army and navy to the cause.

The Battle of Valcour was generally regarded as the first naval battle fought by the U.S. Navy.

LOTS OF FIRSTS came from this region, Dick

thought as he and his companions trudged toward the Ferris homestead. *Dorset, Vermont was one of the first sites of marble quarries. And, Uncle Sam apparently got his start in Troy, New York, in 1812, because of the initials that were printed on supplies destined for the U.S. Army.*

Hmmmm, Dick mumbled. *I wonder where those random thoughts came from?*

***

Chapter 27

Shouts and screams!

The sounds and visions of the desperate naval battle on October 11, 1776, were almost too much for Johnny Vic to bear. He had been so excited at the thought of witnessing the fight. So excited at the thought of seeing the fledgling American Navy in its first battle, he had not considered the death and destruction. The pain. The fear. The loss that had actually occurred.

The air was filled with the shouts of men whose ships had been blown to bits. Filled with the screams of men whose clothing had been set ablaze when barrels of black gunpowder blew up. Filled with the cries of men who had no chance to mourn for their lost friends because they had to continue their own struggles against the maiming forces of fire and cannon balls and flesh-piercing shrapnel.

The Battle of Valcour changed 11-year-old Johnny Vic's opinion of war. It was not exciting. It was terribly painful and frightening. He hoped he would never witness another battle as long as he lived. And so, he was truly glad when he realized there were only a few minutes left on the timer.

"Hey, Dick," he whispered. "We're almost out of

time. We need to get away from these guys."

"Thank God! Let's go. I don't think anyone will notice as long as we're quiet. They're too mesmerized by the battle."

Johnny Vic was already several feet ahead of him and showed no signs of slowing down.

DICK CAUGHT UP with Johnny Vic at the end of the field. He turned for one more glimpse of the raging battle on Lake Champlain. As he did so, he reached for the boy's hand.

"Are you okay? This is quite a nightmare, don't you think?"

"Yes. It is. I never thought about the suffering before. I never thought about the reality of war."

"Many of us don't, Johnny. Too many of us don't." As he spoke, Dick turned away from yet another flash of cannon fire, only to see a different kind of blast–one that was actually a welcomed sight. The air seemed to explode in a colorful cloud that abruptly ended the devastating vision of warfare.

Here we go again, Dick thought. He held his young friend's hand even tighter as they flew through the Metals of Time.

***

Chapter 28

The schooner

Johnny Vic and Dick gently floated onto the deck of a schooner. For a split second, Dick thought, *Oh no, we're on one of the warships!* But he quickly realized he was wrong. It was much too quiet. He turned toward his 11-year-old companion.

"Say, this is much nicer!"

"That's for sure."

"I wonder what boat we're on?"

Johnny Vic laughed. He had already realized they were on a schooner and he remembered what Eric had said.

"Boy, Dick. Don't let anybody hear you call this a boat. They might throw you overboard! It's a schooner."

"A schooner? Like the Lois McLure?"

"Yes, but one of the originals. We probably just jumped into the 1800's."

Johnny Vic scurried toward the bow. "Look," he whispered. "Look at the water! It's so clean and clear. I should collect a sample for Eric."

While Johnny Vic was peering over the side of the schooner, Dick was inspecting their surroundings. He thought, *Well, the crew at the museum certainly did a good job with their replica. This looks just like the real thing.* Then he laughed. *This is the real thing! I can't believe I'm on a real canal schooner, in the 1800's. Linda would love it!*

Dick was still lost in his thoughts when a strong hand clamped onto his shoulder. He also felt the warmth of the man's breath on the back of his neck as he yelled, "Hey Maggie! We got a stowaway! What should I do? Toss 'em to the fish?"

Dick froze.

"Don't you do any such thing until you know who ya got and why they's here, Robert."

Robert immediately released his grip on Dick. "So now, Mr., I sure would like to know what yer doin' on my schooner."

"I can explain," Dick croaked, even as his brain scrambled for a logical story.

"Wait! He's helping me!"

Dick could have kissed the boy. Johnny Vic stepped forward and fibbed, "Some real mean guys almost kidnapped me, and then I thought it would be a good idea. To get away on a ship, I mean. And Dick, here," he pointed toward his friend, "Dick wouldn't let me travel alone."

"Well, I should say not!" came the gravelly voice of the woman called Maggie. "It's not proper for a young thing like yourself to be traveling alone. You never know what you'll be running into. Thieves! Or Gypsies! Or bears, even!"

"Yes," Johnny Vic said, his head bobbing agreeably.

Maggie poked Robert. "So, my man, why don't you mind your manners and ask our friends here if they would like some stew? I have plenty more in the kettle." Without waiting for him to comply, she took Johnny Vic by the hand and waved for Dick to follow. "I'm sure you boys are hungry."

***

Chapter 29

Pirates? Good grief!

Robert and Maggie decided to set anchor early so they could entertain their unexpected guests. "Besides," Robert had said, "there's some mending I should do on the sails before we go much farther up the lake."

Johnny Vic and Dick fished while Robert adjusted his rigging. Maggie spent her time running back and forth from her tiny galley kitchen to tempt her guests with muffins and soup. But when the night was still early, she tossed them each a blanket and bid them goodnight. They were on their own to find whatever comfort they could on the deck.

"We rise with the sun," she confided as she grabbed Robert and said goodnight.

Dick was disappointed that he had not had a chance to question the couple about their life. *Darned woman was like a bouncing ball,* he groused. *Going up and down, up and down. Or maybe she's more like a yo-yo.* He mentioned his musings to Johnny Vic, who giggled and said, "I didn't see any string attached to her, so I guess she isn't a yo-yo."

WHEN THE GAUZY GLOW of the Milky Way disappeared with the onset of the first rays of the sun, Dick was still wide awake. He reached for the helmet that Johnny Vic was clutching even in his sleep, and carefully checked the timer. They soon would be sucked into the vortex that Johnny Vic called the Metals of Time.

Dick listened to the gentle waves that lapped at the belly of the Maggie Rob; and every now and then he heard the splash of a fish that leaped out of the water to grab a passing insect.

Now this could be the good life, Dick thought. *Well, it could, if it were a bit more comfortable.* He shifted with effort. His body was stiff after so many hours on the hard surface of the deck. *Darned hard!* He thought. *I'll never again believe that pine is a "soft" wood.*

Dick remembered that the deck of these schooners was usually made from white pine. *I think the masts and booms were made from white spruce,* his thoughts rambled. *And the hull is probably made from white oak. At least, that's what I think they said at the museum.* He shifted again and his thoughts drifted back to the Lake Champlain Maritime Museum and its staff. He and Linda had enjoyed every minute of their visit.

Dick shivered and snugged his jacket tighter to his body. He tried to forget the discomfort by reviewing his memory of their trip to the museum. *I think these canal schooners could carry a hundred tons of cargo–120 tons tops. And they were almost ninety feet long–88 feet tops.* He wondered what this schooner had carried over the years. *Dry goods, like flour? Or perhaps tea or linens? Or apples?*

Dick was becoming sleepy as he continued his musings about Maggie and Robert and their cargo and their life on the lake. Groggily he wondered if their boat had ever been robbed. He giggled. *Pirates on Lake Champlain? No way. But, then again, with our luck . . . .*

Dick tried to fall asleep, but he just couldn't. He felt uneasy. And then, he realized why.

Good Lord! Those splashes aren't from jumping fish! With a great deal of effort, he forced himself to his feet and peered across the foggy surface of the lake. *Oh no! Somebody's coming and they're being awfully sneaky about it!*

***

Chapter 30

Lake Pirates!

Dick woke Johnny Vic. "Hey, wake up!" he whispered. "We might be in for some trouble!" Then he scuttled toward the ladder that led to the lower deck. He had to alert Maggie and Robert.

He then joined Johnny Vic who was crouching behind a large coil of rope. They watched as Robert and Maggie Krenshaw faced the would-be thieves who had just reached the starboard side of their schooner. They both were aiming rifles at the intruders.

"Okay, you scoundrels, you can turn right around now," Robert shouted, "and go on your way. If you do, we'll forget we ever saw your sorry faces." He shook his gun for emphasis and growled, "So get on with you now, or we'll shoot. And I mean right now, or you'll become food for the fish!"

Johnny Vic admired both Robert and Maggie for their courage. He knew they were tough. Shipping goods up and down the lake and canal was not an easy task. And as he watched them, something that had been nagging at his memory suddenly surfaced with clarity. *Jeepers, she looks a lot like Sue Clark!* He made a mental note to ask his modern-day friend if the Krenshaw name was in her family tree.

As he was thinking about the uncanny resemblance, a sudden gust of wind shifted the sail. He stumbled and fell onto the deck where he spied a small wooden object. *Hey! It's the schooner that Robert was carving!* He picked it up and showed it to Dick.

"Not now, Johnny Vic. I'll look at it later."

Johnny Vic shoved the small wooden carving into his pocket. *I'll give it back to Robert before our timer runs out,* he thought.

Angry snorts and curses could be heard from the intruders; but, as thieves often are, they were too cowardly to challenge their victims face to face, especially when rifles were already aimed at them. They grabbed their oars and rowed. Hard.

And this time, they did not try to hide the sound of their paddles as they sliced through the water.

***

Chapter 31

Home again

The air exploded and Dick and Johnny Vic were once again being propelled through the Metals of Time. *Hooray!* Dick thought. *Piece of cake! I could get used to this!* Just then, he felt a tickle in his nose and he pulled his hand away from his grip on Johnny Vic. The boy stared at him with alarm and tried to shout a warning that they should not move much or allow much space to separate them. But Dick could not hear the warning; no sound could be heard during these journeys through time.

Dick was about to learn that the force of movement within the Metals of Time was greatly enhanced to the point where the swing of an arm can propel one across the vortex. He spun out of control, losing sight of the boy just as the light appeared at the end of the tunnel. *Okay, I remember the light,* he thought. *It's where we get dropped off.* Then he looked around. *Where's Johnny Vic?*

JOHNNY VIC THOUGHT, *Oh no! I wonder how far apart we'll be when we drop out of here? What am I going to tell Linda? What am I gonna tell Uncle Ben?* He was rapidly approaching the light, so he carefully prepared himself for his landing. His feet touched the ground and he took a few wobbly steps even as he scanned his surroundings.

"Oh, good! I'm not far from the cabin at all! But, I wonder where Dick is?" He called Dick's name, but there was no response.

"Dick!" he shouted again. "Nothing, darn it!"

Johnny Vic was about to give up when he heard Bill Clark's deep baritone.

"Hey, Bill! I'm here! I'm okay!"

The big man strode toward the boy. "Your uncle's worried sick . . . where have you been, young man?"

"I, umh, I guess I got carried away when I was down on the shore." *Not too much of a fib,* he thought. *I really was 'carried away.'* He added, "I'm really sorry, Bill. I didn't mean to cause any trouble."

"Well, I'm not the one you need to apologize to. You'd better find your uncle right away." He swung his arm and said, "He just brought Dick to the cabin."

"Poor guy's got a big ol' bop on the head."

"Really? Is he okay?"

"I'm sure he'll be fine in no time. Just a little disoriented, if you know what I mean."

"Thank God!"

Bill gave the boy a quizzical look, then grumbled, "Scoot, you little rascal. Go tell your uncle you're okay. I'll be following right behind you."

"Sure thing, Bill!"

JOHNNY VIC HAD REACHED the top step when Ben burst through the door.

"Thank God you're all right! Where have you been? I thought I was going to have to call out another search party for you!"

"I'm sorry, Uncle Ben. I just lost track of time, I guess."

"Well, no harm done, but try to be more careful, Johnny Vic. Promise me that, okay? I was afraid the storm would come before we found you. It's supposed to be a bad one."

"I promise, Uncle Ben, but what storm are you talking about? I've never seen you so worried about a thunder storm."

"It's more than a thunder storm, Johnny Vic. It's a hurricane. This area will be hit by the tail end of hurricane Serina in a couple of hours, so we have to batten up the hatches so to speak, and head away from it. Bill and Sue have a friend a hundred miles from here who has agreed to take us all in. So, now that we've found you, and we're sure that Dick is well enough to travel, we're going to lock up and go."

"Umh, how is he? Dick, I mean. Bill said he hit his head or something."

"Yeah. He got a good whollop. And it's the funniest thing. He keeps mumbling about Indians and gold and Benedict Arnold. And he also mentioned your name." Ben gave his nephew a piercing look. "I don't suppose you know why he's mixing you up with all that historical stuff, do you?"

"Umh, I . . . ."

Just when Johnny Vic was stumbling with his response, Linda appeared.

"Oh, good. You're here! Dick is asking for you, Johnny Vic. Would you please pop in and let him know you're alright?"

"Sure!"

When Johnny Vic strode toward the spare bedroom, he was so rattled, he did not realize that Robert's wood carving had dropped out of his pocket.

Linda picked it up.

"Wait, Johnny. You dropped this little boat. My . . . it's a beautiful carving." With a big smile, she held it up for everyone to see.

Johnny Vic groaned.

Dick moaned, "Oh, my Lord, I was just dreaming about that little thing!"

With a very, very guilty, face-splitting grin, Johnny

Vic simply uttered, "Really?" And then he said, "I found it down at the lake."

BEN HAD BEEN RACING back and forth, loading the car. Finally, he stopped to say, "Okay, guys. Now that Johnny Vic's back and Dick's well enough, we should go. We really must hurry if we want to miss that storm!"

Johnny Vic groaned inwardly, realizing that he'd be losing his chance to search for Isaiah's gold.

Jeepers! He grumbled. *Will Ben bring me back here when the storm's over? Or, maybe I can talk Mom into coming. Now that,* he grinned, *would be a golden opportunity!*

THE END

Columbus!

A Johnny Vic Adventure

by
Ann Rich Duncan

Chapter 1

Ate/eight ... Write/right

Johnny Vic stretched his arm high over his head and called out, "I've got one, Mrs. Johnson! I've got one!" He beamed when his teacher nodded. "Okay," she said. "Give us an example of a heteronym."

"How about, 'I <u>ate</u> my breakfast at <u>eight</u> o'clock this morning'?"

"That's an excellent try, Johnny, but I'm afraid you just gave us an example of words that are called homophones. They sound the same, but they're spelled differently and have different meanings. A heteronym, on the other hand, has the same spelling, but it's pronounced differently. For instance . . ."

At that moment a man's deep voice said, "EksKYOOZE me, but I have a very good EksKYOOSE for being here today. I do think this is a good SUBject, and I'm glad you are willing to subJECT your students to it."

Mrs. Johnson clapped her hands with delight. "That's wonderful, Dr. Bloom!"

With a wave of her hand, the trim teacher ushered the world-renown neurosurgeon toward the front of the classroom. "Children, I'd like you to meet Dr. William

Herman Bloom. He's a retired neurosurgeon. A published author. An accomplished musician. A playwright, and . . ." she smiled brightly, ". . . an expert wordsmith! But that's not all. He's also a history buff who has agreed to talk to us about one of his favorite historical characters: Christopher Columbus. Isn't that right, Dr. Bloom?"

JOHNNY VIC could not control himself. He stood up and said, "Christopher Columbus is awesome! It's like a PREZent to have you preeZENT him to us!"

Jeffrey popped out of his chair to gush, Mrs. Johnson, can we tape this so we proJECT this PRAHject?"

The room suddenly buzzed with voices–each child trying to outdo the others with a new example of a heteronym. "How about perMIT and PERmit?" one boy asked.

"This one's better: rek-ree-A-shun and REE-creation." The little girl in a royal blue pantsuit smiled triumphantly. She had given the biggest word as an example.

MRS. JOHNSON WAS thrilled to see so much enthusiasm, but she knew their distinguished guest was a very busy man with a limited amount of time, so she picked up her 'emergency horn' and gave it three quick squeezes. The children immediately sat down and folded their hands on their desks. At that point the boisterous doctor said, "My goodness. We must reKORD this RECKord-breaking accomplishment!" He turned to the puzzled teacher and explained, "How did you ever train these young people to respond so quickly?"

Johnny Vic chirped, "I guess it's because when we're HERE and we HEAR the horn, we're blown away." He gave a big nod to punctuate his point.

Mrs. Johnson put her hands on her hips and exclaimed, "Johnathan Bradley Victor, THAT was another homophone!" She shook her head and stared at the ceiling. The room exploded with a burst of laughter.

***

Chapter 2

There's more to learn . . . much more!

Dr. Bloom stood in front of Mrs. Johnson's students. He glanced at the clock. He smiled at a shy-looking girl in the front row. He unbuttoned his tweed jacket, hung it on the back of a chair, stretched his arms wide and asked, "What do you see?"

The shy girl picked at an imaginary piece of lint on her butter-yellow sweater, then raised her hand. With big eyes and a voice as soft as a whisper, she asked, "A man who took off his jacket?"

"Yes. But what else do you see?"

"A doctor!" one boy said.

"A guest speaker," shouted a girl with pigtails and bristly bangs that looked like they had been dipped in blue paint.

Dr. Bloom whispered, "Yes. Yes to all of your answers. But, there's more, isn't there? Am I not a husband? A father? A son? A grandson? Am I not also a poet? And . . . I'm a bullfighter! Oh, there's a lot more to me than what you've just been told. And I dare say, the same goes for each of you, too!"

Dr. Bloom pointed at the shy girl, and then at the

boys in the back row before resting his gaze upon Johnny Vic.

"And that's what fascinates me about history. There's more to the people. More to the events. More to the towns and cities, the inventions and conventions. More to everything . . . than what you see or hear in the classroom, in the books, or in the movies." He swept his gaze across the rows of desks and asked, "Who would like to be my guinea pig?" Several hands shot up.

"Me!"

"No, pick me!"

Much to the children's delight, Dr. Bloom closed his eyes and started to sing, "Eenie, meanie, miney, moe, catch a student by the toe . . ." With one arm stretched out like a poker, he twirled around three times and then ended the well-known rhyme, "If they holler, I won't let go, and now, I catch YOU!" His fingered was aimed directly at Johnny Vic.

"Oh boy! What do I do?"

"Well, you can stand tall for a few minutes up here at the front of the room while I choose one more student."

More arms shot into the air. Dr. Bloom twirled again and this time his aim settled upon a boy in the third row. "And what is your name?" he asked with raised brows.

"I'm Kaden."

"Okay, Kaden. Come on up to the front!"

While Kaden was making his way toward the black-board, Dr. Bloom said, "I'm here to tell you about Columbus. But, I think it's important for all of you to understand that everyone is important. You know, you have to believe in yourself before you can truly appreciate others. Do you believe that?"

Johnny Vic replied, "Yessir!"

"Good." Dr. Bloom nodded at Johnny Vic · then turned toward his classmates. "Okay, Johnny is our guinea pig and Kaden is our scribe."

"Scribe?"

"Yes. That is the person who writes down everything that we say."

"Oh." Kaden grabbed a piece of chalk. "Okay, then. I'm ready."

"Good. So, the first thing you should do, Kaden, is write Johnny's name way up high on the left." He pointed to the corner of the blackboard.

Kaden was excited. He wrote with such force that his chalk broke half way through Johnny Vic's name.

"Oops!"

With a red face, he stooped to pick up the broken chalk.

"That's okay, Kaden. I like a man who's forceful." Dr. Bloom watched as Kaden finished writing. "And now, a little to the right, I want you to write 'Columbus'."

"Hey!" Two girls exclaimed in unison. "They're homophones: right and write!"

Other voices chimed in.

"Knight/night!"

"Dew/do!"

"Bite/byte!"

"Knew/new!"

MRS. JOHNSON CLAPPED her hands with delight and Dr. Bloom thought, *these kids are outta' sight!*

***

Chapter 3

We all have greatness in us.

Johnny Vic gave a studious nod when Jessica said he was intelligent. He forced his face into a serious frown and pretended to hold his ground when Sam said he was stubborn. He blushed when Sarah said he was cute. *Gee,* he thought. *I wonder how they'll describe Columbus. I bet they won't say he's cute!"*

"Adventurous," Sam said when they began to describe Christopher Columbus, and Johnny Vic thought, *Heck, I'm just as adventurous as he was–I can travel back through time. That's really adventurous.*

"Stubborn," said Gregory.

Well, I guess that's another thing we both have in common, Johnny Vic thought with a slim grin.

"OKAY NOW, KIDS," Dr. Bloom said. "As you can see, you've described Johnny Vic and Christhoper Columbus with a lot of the same words. And so, you can conclude that they are very similar. And that's important because I believe that you'll be able to relate to Christopher Columbus a lot better if you think of him as a person–a person just like yourself or your friends–a person who can accomplish great things."

He swept one arm in a grand gesture. "And so, I'd like to share with you my findings. My conclusions. My theories. About that great explorer, Cristobel Colon, also known as Cristofero Colombo, but to us, he is Christopher Columbus."

***

Chapter 4

Many hardships–many heroes

Dr. Bloom said, "Picture this: you're in a strange land, far, far away from home. The only food you've been able to eat is the fish and game and berries and leaves that you've plucked from the land and sea." He made eye contact with several of the children in Mrs. Johnson's classroom and thought, *This is wonderful–they're paying attention!*

"You cannot call for help. There are no cell phones. In fact, you've never even heard of a telephone. You cannot look something up on the internet–the computer was not yet invented, either. And you've just been cornered by an angry band of natives. Well, that was just the situation for Christopher Columbus during his fourth voyage. The great Christopher Columbus and about 141 members of his crew. They were marooned on the north shore of the island country we now call Jamaica. As the leader, Columbus felt responsible for everyone's safety. And on this fourth great voyage, the pressure was even greater than usual, because his brother, Bartolomeo, and his 13-year-old son, Fernando, and his close friend, Flesco, were with him. Oh, it was a troubled time, indeed!"

Dr. Bloom paused for a moment to scan the room. He

decided it was time for the kids to get involved in the story.

"Now Benjamin," he said. "Would you please draw a picture of an island on the blackboard? I believe that Christopher Columbus was the greatest navigator of all time and one of mankind's greatest sailors. He was made of stern stuff, with an iron will, a love of God, and . . . he was noble in character."

Dr. Bloom paused again. "So, Benjamin, would you please also draw a picture of a shipwreck?" Scratchy chalk sounds could be heard from the blackboard as the boy worked on his picture.

"You know, children, they talk about the Vikings. How brave and adventurous they were. But, don't forget–the Vikings did not sail far from land. They literally hopped. They hopped from Norway to the Shetlands, to the Faroc Islands, to Iceland, and then they hopped again, to Greenland and to Baffin Island to Vineland–with little more than three or four days between each time they set sail."

As he spoke, Dr. Bloom noticed a wave of smiles and giggles that finally erupted into loud bursts of laughter. He turned toward the blackboard. Benjamin had added action lines to his drawing: the ship appeared to have hopped to the island and instead of sails, it had large rabbit ears and a caption that read, "WANTED: Sails for Sale."

The laughter was contagious. Mrs. Johnson knew she had to get the children to settle down . . . once she could stop her own laughter!

***

Chapter 5

Sailing the ocean blue

Dr. Bloom continued his tale.

"So, that's what we know of the Vikings. And then, you have Christopher Columbus. He deliberately set sail for a goal of 2,600 miles. Twenty six hundred miles! That was unthinkable back in his day, although they were known to travel around 800 miles, to the Canary Islands."

He paused for a moment to look at the youngsters in the front row. "So, do you know when Columbus lived?"

"Yessir," said Annabeth. "He sailed the ocean blue in fourteen hundred and ninety two."

"Very good, that is definitely a well-known fact. But, did you know that he set sail four different times? And, I am going to tell you about one of those journeys. I even have artifacts to show you! One of them was just discovered last year and was given to me by a friend."

He pulled a small blue box from his pocket and opened it up to reveal a small metal object. "This," he said, "is part of an instrument that Columbus may have used on his fourth trip. It was given to me while I was traveling and developing my own theory about that journey. I was the guest of the Spanish Ambassador to the Caribbean . . . at a re-enactment of the landing of the Nina, Pinta and Santa Maria upon the western part of San Salvador Island, in the Bahamas."

Dr. Bloom gazed ahead as fond memories filled his head. He said, "It was the culmination of a 12 million dollar project to study and replicate the famous ships of 1492."

All of the students leaned forward at their desks and gazed with wide-eyed wonder. They were amazed. They thought it would be so exciting to be able to travel along Christopher Columbus' route and they tried to imagine what it would feel like to have been with him.

Johnny Vic's excitement was even more intense. He knew he would be able to experience one of those voyages. *Oh boy! Dr. Bloom is going to stay with me and Uncle Ben tonight! I've just gotta have a chance to lock onto that thing with my metal detector!*

***

Chapter 6

Wow, what a trip!

Dr. Bloom said, "Thank you so much, Ben. You've served a wonderful meal and I've enjoyed this interview immensely. But now, I'm ready to say goodnight. Again, I do appreciate your hospitality."

"My pleasure, Dr. B. My pleasure."

Johnny Vic jumped from his seat. "You were great today, Dr. Bloom. All my friends loved your talk, they really did."

"Thank you, my boy. I'm glad they enjoyed my visit. It was great fun for me, too."

"But, before we go to bed, could I see your artifacts again? Please . . .!"

"Why certainly. As a matter of fact, I'll go one better. You can hold on to them until the morning. Would you like that?"

Although the wise doctor knew that his collection of artifacts would fuel the fire of the boy's imagination, he did not know that they would also propel them both on an unforgettable journey back through time to actually see Christopher Columbus!

DR. BLOOM CRACKED his bedroom window open–he loved to sleep with fresh country air wafting across his face. As a matter of fact, he often joked to his patients that a brisk country breeze was the best sleeping aid a person could buy. He took several deep breaths and completed twenty rounds of his nightly stretching exercises. He then reached again for the window. *That breeze is so delightful,* he thought, *"I think I'll open it all the way.*

After clicking his bedside lamp off, Dr. Bloom discovered that he had a clear view of the starlit sky. His eyes opened wide and he whipped his covers off, then padded to the window. "Marvelous!" he exclaimed. Cassiopeia, the widened W created by five stars that etched themselves across the milky way, was shining brightly. He snatched a cozy fleece jogging suit from his suitcase and crossed toward the door. With a sudden snap of his fingers he grabbed his sneakers, thinking it might be a good night for a walk.

JOHNNY VIC WAS already on the lawn, inches away from the patio that Dr. Bloom was heading for; and as soon as he saw the guest room plunge into darkness, he placed Dr. Bloom's treasures onto the ground. *Darned helmet,* he growled, struggling to put it on. When it finally snapped into place, he looked up at the starry sky.

"Christopher Columbus, here I come," he murmured before switching his metal detector on and aiming it toward the artifacts. One of them was an old key that Dr. Bloom's friend had claimed was the one that had been used to free Columbus from his chains of imprisonment.

"Why, Johnny Vic–what are you doing out here in the darkness?" Dr. Bloom asked.

"Oh no! Don't come any closer Dr. Bloom–you can't!" Johnny Vic was horrified. Swirling bolts of light were already zooming around them.

A NEARBY RABBIT leaped to safety seconds before it saw the humans disappear. At the edge of the yard, her mate spun his gaze toward the commotion, then scratched an ear and resumed his hungry inspection of Ben's vegetable garden. One hop brought him within reach of a delicious patch of tender green carrot tops.

***

Chapter 7

With a fuzzy head, Dr. Bloom mumbled, "What just happened?"

He was desperately trying to analyze the events of the last few minutes.

"Well, I saw a lot of colorful lightning bolts, and I think I've heard some of my stroke patients give similar descriptions." He wiggled his fingers.

"Good! I haven't lost the use of my arms or hands." He then flexed his legs and wriggled his toes and almost shouted, "My legs are okay, too! But if it wasn't a stroke, what just happened to me?"

Johnny Vic gulped and said a silent prayer. He was glad that Dr. Bloom had survived the magical trip through the Metals of Time. He trotted toward the confused man.

"Umh . . . Dr. Bloom? Umh, I can tell you what just happened."

"You can?"

"Yes. And I'm sorry, I'm really sorry, honest! I didn't know you were there! I never would have turned it on if I knew you were there."

"Slow down, lad. You never would have turned

WHAT on? Are you saying you caused this? Whatever it is? How? What? Speak up, boy . . ."

"Well, it was my . . . umh, it was my metal detector."

"Your metal detector? What . . . did it explode?"

"Sort of. But, well, not exactly."

"It sort of exploded but did not exactly explode?"

"Exactly. And well, I think we're now probably in the 1400's or maybe the 1500's.

"The fourteen or fifteen hundred what?"

Johnny Vic swallowed. Hard.

"Come now, my boy. Don't take a century to explain yourself."

"Well, it's just that . . . well, that's it!"

"What's 'it?'"

"The century! I'm talking about the century we're now in! My metal detector has brought us back to the fourteen hundreds . . . or the fifteen hundreds. We're in the time of Columbus, Dr. B!"

***

Chapter 8

The settlement

Christopher Columbus stared at the horizon from his perch at the edge of the sea. Salty water lapped at the boulders below him then withdrew to make way for a new wave to flow in. In a rare moment of self doubt, he lamented his plight. "Glory be to my God in heaven, what has my ambition wrought?" He was thinking about the day when he and his crew had been forced to bring their crippled craft to its final resting place on the shore several miles to the south.

Like skeletal remains with ribs exposed, the ship had been partially dismantled; its sails, no longer the proud white badge of an ambitious fleet whose voyage had been destined to change the world. Once able to capture the power of the wind to bring him and his men to the ends of the earth, the damaged sailcloth was cut into pieces and stretched, like animal pelts, to dry on the beach. Every inch of material that could be salvaged was stripped from the ship and used to create a shelter. Columbus mourned for his ship. He thought, *like flowers that blaze gloriously in the summer sun, only to wither and die and become the food for their own roots.* He sighed, *"I guess everything has its day . . . 'from dust to dust'* he quoted sadly.

Not one to remain sullen for long, Christopher Columbus inhaled a big breath of salty air and shook off the sadness. He had work to do. He had a crew to protect. A mission to complete. And at the sound of footsteps and shouts, he turned away from the sea.

THE RACING FOOTSTEPS startled Johnny Vic. He dropped closer to his fellow time traveler. A grizzled sailor was racing toward the man on the beach. *Wow,* Johnny thought. *That guy up there looks just the pictures I've seen of Christopher Columbus. This must be one of his men coming.*

Dr. Bloom recognized the language and he did his best to translate what he heard. "Admiral!" the man had shouted. "Admiral! I've seen the savages. Their huts are a good mile away. We have brought two of them here with us!"

"A mile you say?"

"Aye, sir. That's all."

"Well then, we'll have to be ready to defend ourselves if we must." He knew that it would only be a matter of time before the natives found their encampment. He turned toward his friend.

"Flesco, you'll have to find assistance for us as soon as you can. I have spoken to Diego and while you were gone, he fashioned this vessel for your journey. You must load it up and go swiftly to the Governor. And take some of these savages with you, too."

Columbus then joined his other two men and said, "We must return to the shelter and build it up. Make ready for an attack. And we have to tally our weaponry." He turned toward Flesco and said, "And may God grant you safe journey, my good friend."

Dr. Bloom heard a chorus of, "Aye, sir," and he felt glad that he had recently brushed up on his Spanish. He decided the shelter they were talking about was the settlement they had been forced to build after their ship had been wrecked. *I cannot believe my ears, or my mind,* he scoffed. *Do I really believe I'm watching Christopher*

Columbus and his men? He glanced at his young companion.

"1400's . . . right, Dr. Bloom?"

"Well, possibly 1502, or 1503," he replied and with a resounding plop, he sat on a nearby rock.

***

Chapter 9

A scary journey

Even from their distant perch, Johnny Vic and Dr. Bloom could see that the men they were watching were frightened and emotionally distraught.

"I know I must be dreaming," Dr. Bloom whispered, "but, I think we are witnessing the start of that journey I told you about–where Flesco and Diego sail their canoe to Hispaniola! I had always envisioned it to be a poignant moment." He looked at Johnny Vic. "Do you know what poignant means?"

"Yessir. Sort of. It's like really, really emotional and intense, right?"

"You got it." He smiled and returned his gaze to the men on the shore.

FLESCO STARED AT Bartolomeo, his friend and brother of Christopher Columbus. Even from a distance one could sense the fierce emotional ties. It was as though each man was etching the sight of the other into his memory for eternity–as if they feared they would not see each other again. Ever.

Eyes glowed with unshed tears. Hands trembled.

Prayers were uttered. Love. Respect. Fear. Naked emotions for all to see. *We're witnessing the farewell of real men, true heroes,* thought Dr. Bloom. *There is no room here for egos or treachery.*

Flesco turned to face the 'vessel' that he and the other men would be traveling in. It was a large canoe. He thought, *I do not want to travel these treacherous waters in such a craft. But, I will follow my beloved friend's orders.* He made the sign of the cross and gestured for the natives to seat themselves. He then gave Diego Mendez a nod and they shoved the little craft into the water. He looked up at the bright blue sky and down toward the sparkling water before jumping into the boat.

Diego Mendez, the Spanish explorer who would some day make his own appearance in the history books, looked at Christopher Columbus' friend. "You are not happy to make this voyage? Why not, Flesco?"

"It is true. I am not. For two reasons: first, I am fearful for the admiral. The men are angry. They may turn against him. And the natives are no longer friendly toward us. And this journey! Tell me, how are we to find our way to Hispaniola in this? And return in time to save all of our men?"

"We can only do what we can do."

"You are correct, Diego. And may God bless our mission." At that moment, an unexpected swell threatened to engorge their tiny boat. The natives remained crouched on their seats, more frightened of their captors than of the merciless walls of water that were tossing them about. Flesco had misgivings about the little craft, but he was grateful for Diego's ingenuity. He had attached a wooden guard on the front end to stave off the waves. He had also pitched and greased the craft and added a wooden rudder to make it as seaworthy as possible.

AS THE HOURS PASSED, the men suffered from the blazing heat and the erratic winds and currents. Several times, Flesco felt the need to thank his Lord for protecting them. He prayed for their safety, and for the safety of Christopher Columbus, Bartolomeo and all of the men.

"Please look out for all of their men, my Lord God. I trust that You will give my great friend and his brother the wisdom to prevail as they all wait for our return." Flesco had already heard many mumblings and grumblings . . . hints of mutiny!

He estimated that he and his companions had traveled almost half way through their journey when he flipped the canvas that covered their meager store of provisions. They were already running out of food and they had no more water. They had been battling the heat, the wind, the rain, and the relentless waves for days.

Flesco was exhausted. He did not know how long he had been staring at the endless waterway before them when his eyes widened with delight. "Diego! Look! Land ahead on the starboard side!"

Flesco had spied a rocky outcrop of land that was situated off the west coast of the southern peninsula of Haiti. He pulled the parchment that he had been keeping safely hidden in his coat. It was a crude map of Cuba, Jamaica and Hispanoila, drawn by Christopher Columbus.

It is hard to believe that my good friend and commander had earned a living as a map maker. He had drawn this one in such a hurry! Cuba looks like a snake, Jamacia looks like the wings of a tiny angel and Hispaniola looks like a turtle–a smashed turtle at that! Flesco's smile quickly disappeared when he bent closer to study the path they were taking.

On the map, it looked like a short, easy trip. But Flesco knew better. He and his companions were traveling through 40 leagues of dangerous waters. *A 40-league nightmare of violent currents and unpredictable wind. May our Lord God continue to protect us!*

"Diego," Flesco said. "According to my calculations, we have made half the journey. We surely will survive the rest of the way–if we can find water here!" He licked his lips. They were cracked and bleeding. He knew none of them would last much longer without water to drink. He knew that even a few drops could mean the difference between life and death for all of them.

The natives had seen the distant shoreline as well and they renewed their paddling with vigor. When they reached the land, Flesco jumped into the water and tied them off. The other men then scrambled out of the boat and they all staggered across the rocky ground to search for fresh water. Soon they spied a crevice high upon the cliff that was filled with the precious liquid–*rain water!*

One of the natives dove toward the pool in response to Flesco's excitement. He was horrified. He tried to stop the man. "No!" he cried. "No! You must not drink too much too quickly when you have been without water so long! It will kill you as surely as the blazing sun!"

The man did not understand Flesco's words. He thought the Spaniard was trying to save all of the water for himself and he greedily gulped as much as he could. Flesco dropped to his knees and prayed for the man. Diego had already seized another native, while the others watched with puzzled expressions. Diego held the native tightly and Flesco pressed a damponed rag to his parched lips. With desperate gestures, he tried to tell the others to go slow.

Moments later they all understood. The native who drank greedily from the pool had dropped to the ground. He was holding his stomach and writhing in pain. He knew nothing about dehydration, nothing about an imbalance of electrolytes. He was simply feeling the devastating effect of drinking too much water too soon after going without it for far too long. He would not survive.

FLESCO AND DIEGO and their companions traveled another 20 miles until they came to Hispanoila. They used a few coins to purchase food and clothing and labored to make themselves presentable for the Governor. But, they need not have hurried. They were soon to learn that Comendador Don Nicolas deOrando was no friend to Cristobel Colon. He continually delayed his promises to meet with Flesco and Diego, and several months passed before he finally agreed to send a ship to rescue the wayward explorer and his crew.

*   *   *

Chapter 10

The eclipse

$\mathbf{F}$ear gripped thousands of hearts one moonlit night in 1504, including a handful of natives who were threatening Christopher Columbus. However, Johnny Vic and Dr. Bloom were not afraid. They were watching the notorious explorer at his craftiest! He was using his knowledge of science and the heavens as leverage against the natives.

"That was scary for a while, huh, Dr. B?"

"Yes. It certainly was. I do believe the natives were reluctant to continue providing food for them."

THE TWO TIME TRAVELERS were hiding in a crevice that offered a clear view of the incident. They could not hear what was being said, but Dr. Bloom knew the story well. He understood by the great man's gestures that he was telling them his God would be displeased and make the moon go away if they refused to help him and his men.

CHRISTOPHER COLUMBUS whispered to his brother, Bartholomew, "Our God is certainly with us tonight, Bart–by bringing these savages to us at this particular time. I do not believe they have an understanding of the heavens. I am certain they do not know that we will experience an eclipse of the moon tonight. We can use it to our advantage!"

"Chris–I pray that you are correct."

"I am, my dear brother. I believe that I am." He turned to face the dark-skinned men and pointed toward the sand. He fell to his knees and used his fingers to etch a simple line drawing of his ship and men and the hills and trees of the island, with a circular moon hovering above them. He made eye contact with several of the natives and pointed at the real moon. Then he pointed toward his picture before aiming his blazing gaze at them again.

The natives nodded and raised their hands in question. They seemed to be asking, *Why are you showing us what we already know?*

Columbus then drew eyes and a smile, high above the moon and tried his best to indicate that they were the eyes of his God–a God who was pleased. He then drew a stick figure of a native who had killed a sailor with a spear. The Godly smile quickly changed to a frown.

After making sure that the natives were following his story, Columbus drew a line directly from the angry eyes to the moon before smearing the sand and making it disappear. The natives began to mumble. Christopher Columbus hid his own sly grin as he replaced the attacking native with a friendly one offering gifts. The Godly face then smiled and the sandy moon reappeared.

Columbus stood up, stared directly into the eyes of the native leaders and raised his hands while murmuring words of a prayor.

The natives raised their spears, ready to respond, but suddenly, the moon disappeared!

Several of the natives screamed. Others dropped to their knees in surrender.

THE STORY QUICKLY SPREAD. Awestruck, the natives repeatedly returned with gifts of food, drink, clothing and tools.

Columbus and his men were safe.
For now.

***

Chapter 11

Here comes trouble!

Johnny Vic checked the timer on his cap. They had less than ten minutes before it would transport them to their next adventure. He thought about the artifacts that set off the journey. He decided the knife must have sent them to witness the eclipse. He hoped the key would bring them to Castile. *It should,* he thought. *That is where he and his brothers were sent when they were shackled in those chains!*

He whispered to Dr. Bloom.

"Hey, Dr. B. What do you know about his imprisonment? Do you think the key in your box was really the one they used when Christopher Columbus was put into prison?"

Dr. Bloom cleared his throat and whispered, "I believe so, Johnny. I have no reason to doubt my friend. He seemed sincere. But, then again, it could very well be the key to anything–a box, a door, a cell. Most anything, I expect."

"Tell me that story, Dr. B."

"Well, okay. I'd be glad to, but first, Johnny Vic, I want you to tell me what you know about Christopher Columbus." The sly doctor was curious to see if the boy had been paying attention to his lecture. He suspected that Johnny Vic had been daydreaming about the possibility of going on this adventure.

"Well, let me see." Johnny Vic scrunched his brows and searched his memory. Then his eyes lit up. He was ready to show off his knowledge.

"Okay . . . I remember that he called one of his settlements, "Navidad," which is the Spanish word for Christmas! It was in what we now call Haiti."

He furrowed his brow again.

"Hmmm. What else do I remember?" He tapped his chin, then proceeded with a fast-paced narration.

"Well, he was born in 1451, in Genoa, Italy, and was named after Saint Christopher, the protector of travelers. The name actually means, "Bringing the story of Christ to other people." He left on his first voyage in August of 1492, after King Ferdinand and Queen Isabella ordered the people of Palos to give him three ships. And wasn't it the Santa Maria that tore its bottom eventually? So they tore it apart to build a fort? That was also in Haiti, right?" Johnny Vic furrowed his brows again. "But, I think we're watching him on his fourth voyage, when he was stranded in Jamaica. Yeah, that makes sense. The eclipse he used occurred on February 29, in 1504. I remember the date, cause it was a leap year."

Johnny Vic snapped his tiny flashlight on and held up a power bar.

"Want a bite, Dr. Bloom?" He put the end of his flashlight into his mouth, aimed it toward the sweet treat and tore at the wrapper. Moments later, his eyes lit up again.

"Oh, yeah! His name, in Spanish, was Cristobel Colon. And in Genoa he was known as Cristofero Colombo. And during his first voyage, on October 12th, 1492, he named an island, San Salvador. Named it after Jesus, didn't he?"

"Very good, young man. Very goooo . . ."

Dr. Bloom's brows shot up and he croaked, "Oh, dear. We might be in trouble now!"

One of the natives had seen the beam from the flashlight. He was racing toward them with his spear raised high.

***

Chapter 12

Genoa

Johnny Vic's heart raced and he blinked with uncertainty. He thought that this trip through the Metals of Time was taking a lot longer than his previous trips. *Jeepers! I hope we're not stuck here forever! But, I am glad we got sucked away before that spear got hurled at us.*

Dr. Bloom, on the other hand, was enjoying himself immensely. He was wondering where they would land and if it would still pertain to the life of his hero, Christopher Columbus. His mind raced from one Columbus story to another. He thought about the key that was in the box that Johnny Vic's metal detector had locked onto.

I still do not believe we are traveling through time, yet there is no other logical explanation; but, if we are, I do hope the key will bring us to the time when Christopher Columbus was released from his bondage in those dreadful irons.

Dr. Bloom tried to visualize the scene.

Let's see now, it was during his third voyage, that began on May 30, 1498, that he was put in chains and ordered back to Cadize. He had just finished his suppression of the rebels in the Concepcion de la Vega. Francisco de Bobadilla had sent the order on behalf of the King and Queen as part of his mission to dispense what they called, "royal justice." Christopher and two of his brothers had been arrested and put in chains.

And, I like this part–the captain of the ship that was bringing them to Castile offered to undo his chains, but Columbus said, "No." He was certainly made of stern stuff. I think it shows just how honorable he was! He believed he had been put in chains in the name of the Soverigns and he should wear them until they gave the order for removal.

How aweful! Dr. Bloom thought. He looked at his own wrists and tried to imagine how it would feel to have cold, hard, possibly even rusty, shackles on them. *Shackles that would rub against the skin, causing bruises and God only knows what.*

He closed his eyes and shivered. Moments later, he felt something touch his arm. Through the slits of his eyes, Dr. Bloom saw Johnny Vic. The boy had grabbed him and was pointing toward a light that was barely visible.

"That must be where we get off!" Dr. Bloom exclaimed, but his excitement went unnoticed. Sound did not exist in the Metals of Time.

JOHNNY VIC AND Dr. Bloom landed on a grassy knoll with a soft thud. *Finally!* Johnny Vic thought. *We made it.*

He twirled around with excitement. "Dr. B.! We must be in Genoa? Or Spain? Or Portugal? Or someplace like that! Look at the ocean! Look at the grass! Look at those buildings!"

Boxy stone columns and high rounded arches created a breathtaking scene, with the bright blue sky as a backdrop. Each column was made from alternating light and dark stones. Johnny Vic wondered how people could have built such immense structures and cut the huge stones so perfectly without power tools. He twirled around again.

"Holy smokes, look at that guy over there." He

hoped he was looking at Flesco. *After all, Flesco was supposed to be the last person who actually touched that key before enclosing it in the little box.*

Dr. Bloom was still staring when the man finally noticed them. He held his hand above his eyes, probably to shield them from the bright sunlight, and sauntered across the field toward them.

Dr. Bloom tried his Spanish. "Hello. I am Dr. William Bloom and this is my young companion, Johnny Vic."

The man stared at them with furrowed brow. He wondered, *Who is this man and boy in the strange garb?* But he said, "Have you traveled far? What brings you to my land?"

"We heard such great things about your city. We wished to see Genoa for ourselves."

"You are very kind to say so."

Dr. Bloom shrugged.

"How did you arrive? I did not hear about any ships coming to port today."

"We . . . this . . . umh, this is not our first day at port."

"I see. Then you must have traveled on the Genoan Queen? You are lucky to be alive. It is not the best seafaring vessel, I understand."

"Quite so."

Dr. Bloom let the stranger lead the conversation. His ability to understand the spoken word was far better than his ability to speak it.

"Have you found a place to stay? Of course, probably not." He seemed to be talking to himself, then looked up and said, "Please forgive my poor manners and allow me to introduce myself. I am Humberto Mendigo. I would be honored if you would come with me to my home. Actually, it is not my own home, I am a servant for Bartolomeo Fieschi. I live in his father's home. I can see that you are fed and that you have clean beds to sleep in. Shall we go?" He gestured toward a path on his left before saying, "I will send someone to pick up your baggage later."

Dr. Bloom thought, *What luck! It is not Flesco as I had hoped, but we may get to meet him after all! I cannot believe we are going to be guests in his family home!* He glanced at Johnny Vic and hoped the timer was on a short fuse and that they would be on their way home before Humberto realized they had not arrived on that ship!

***

Chapter 13

Look! They have pomegranates!

Johnny Vic whispered, "Wow, look at this place, Dr. B.! It's a castle! A real castle!"

"It certainly is, my boy."

Humberto led them through the wide arch and asked them to remain there until he returned.

"So, who is he and what did he say, Dr. B.?"

"He said he's a servant who works for Flesco's family. He's invited us to stay with them, so he must have some influence here. He must be of a profession that is highly regarded."

"I didn't know that Flesco lived in a castle."

"He did, my boy. He certainly did. His family had a lot of power . . . for 200 years or so, I believe. They were quite proud of the fact that they had about 50 cardinals and two popes in their family tree. Their influence was highly valued by Christopher Columbus. Quite an asset for him, actually. But they knew him as Christoforo Colombo."

Humberto returned to his whispering guests. He stared at them in puzzlement. *They speak a strange language, but I believe I heard them mention my friend's name.* He said, "You speak of my friend, Cristofero?"

"Why yes, we have heard about his efforts to sail around the world."

"Yes, he has great ambitions. He has accomplished much. He is the son of Domenico Colombo, the guardian of the East Gate, here in Genoa."

Dr. Bloom could see the light of pride flicker in the man's eyes.

ANOTHER SERVANT approached. Humberto said, "Adolfo–run to the cook and ask for drink and some cake for my guests. And on your way, ask Ronaldo to come. He must show them to the beds in the guest quarters. Now, hurry!"

He then held his arms in welcome. "Please, follow me to the piazza. You can wait there for your food and drink."

Humberto's sandals flopped along the tiles of the dimly lit corridor until they passed through a sun drenched courtyard. It was filled with plant life. *A botanical wonder!* Dr. Bloom thought. He tapped Johnny Vic on the shoulder and whispered, "Look there! They have pomegranates. Just like the scene in that story I read to your classmates."

Johnny Vic was feeling hungry. He hoped they would be able to eat something before the timer went off again. Humberto ushered them to a table and apologized, saying he could not join them, he had to return to his duties. The two time travelers were ravenous and they enjoyed a feast of freshly baked bread, cold meats, goat cheese, and round, pale fruits that tasted remarkably like oranges. Dr. Bloom explained that they actually were oranges.

"The oranges we know in our own time," he whispered, "are all injected with orange dye." Johnny Vic's eyes opened wide with surprise. "I didn't know that," he whispered back. He had just finished his second helping of bread when the timer buzzed.

Johnny Vic felt lucky. His stomach was full and no one was with them when the air ignited with a thousand bolts of color and sound.

THEY WERE NOT going home yet, though. They were about to experience the scariest part of their journey!

***

Chapter 14

A stormy sea!

Unfortunately, Johnny Vic and Dr. Bloom slipped out of the Metals of Time, into the middle of a terrifying storm at sea!

Johnny Vic had never been so afraid! The noise was deafening! Wave after wave crashed over them–each one threatening to topple the little ship. Lighning lit up the scene with flash after flash, each revealing a psychedelic nightmare. He saw two wooden crates topple into the turbulent sea as he clutched a heavy metal chain.

Flash! A sudden glimpse of Dr. Bloom, clutching the same chain. Each of them was praying for the other's safety, and they had yet to even realize where they were! What ship were they on? What century were they in?

AND FINALLY, ANOTHER blinding flash of lightning illuminated the sky, the tumbling ship, and two members of its crew. *Thank you God!* Thought Johnny Vic.

Dr. Bloom was also expressing his thanks to the Creator. He heard one of the men utter through clenched teeth, "So, Chris, you have dreamed of captaining a ship? How does this feel? My leg may be broken. You must take charge!"

"Christo? Oh, my heaven on earth! It's him again! I just know it's him!" Dr. Bloom realized that he and Johnny Vic were witnessing another exciting day in the life of Christopher Columbus. It was the day that Dr. Bloom believed had marked the man's destiny. He was in his late teens. He and his friend, Flesco, had gone sailing and had been taken by surprise by this sudden storm. Dr. Bloom thought, Hmmmm. *That voice sounds familiar. I'll bet it's Humberto. Makes sense!*

He was no longer afraid. *After all,* he reasoned, *Columbus, Flesco, and their two adult companions had all survived the storm.* He was certain that he and Johnny Vic would, also. He tried to get the boy's attention.

"Don't worry, Johnny Vic!" he shouted. "We are with Christopher Columbus! This time he's a young lad!"

Johnny Vic saw that Dr. Bloom was trying to talk to him, but the storm drowned out his voice. He only caught a few words, but then, he saw the good doctor was holding his thumb up in a gesture of success. *Jeepers!* He thought. *He doesn't seem to be afraid anymore. I wonder why?*

Johnny Vic returned his own thumbs up. *I don't want him to worry about me,* he thought. Then he saw that Dr. Bloom was pointing toward the front of the ship. That is when he realized why the good doctor was no longer afraid. The storm was losing its power and two men were finally gaining control.

One of the men limped across the deck and ordered young Christopher Columbus to shorten sail. He then contrived a jury rig for the rudder, thus enabling the small ship to stagger toward home.

LIKE FRIGHTENED CRABS, Dr. Bloom and Johnny Vic scooted across the slippery deck on their hands and bent legs. They were trying to scuttle behind a pile of debris, but, Humberto saw them and shouted, "Halt! In the name of all that is dear to Genoa, name yourselves!" He turned toward his friend. "We have stowaways, captain!

What should we do?"

The boat suddenly tossed to and fro and the man screamed in agony. A thick coil of rope had fallen on his bad leg.

Ever the quick wit, Dr. Bloom blurted, in Spanish, "I can fix his leg!" He scrambled to the ailing man's aid.

"Okay, sir, bite this and hold your breath." He had given the sailor a piece of wood to place between his teeth. And without warning, he yanked on the leg. The man yelped, then fell silent.

As Johnny Vic watched Dr. Bloom in action, he noticed a scrap of parchment that had been caught in the ropes. He stuffed it into his pocket as Dr. Bloom tore his own shirt off and used it to tie a second piece of wood as a splint. The doctor then stood and said, "He should not walk on that leg for 40 days. Then he will be healed."

Christopher Columbus stared at the stranger with mixed emotions. He was glad that Flesco's guard would be healed. *Flesco? Great God in heaven! Where is my little friend?*

Columbus shouted, "Flesco! Flesco? Where are you? Are you alive? Have you escaped harm?"

A muffled voice could be heard. "Yes, I am without harm, Chris, but I am trapped! I cannot lift these vessels and containers away. You must help me if you can!"

Christopher Columbus scrambled past Johnny Vic toward the rail where a flight of stairs led to the lower deck. Dr. Bloom absentmindedly wondered if that was the level that was called the 'waist' in Columbus' day.

"I am coming, Flesco. I am coming."

As he climbed down the stairs, Christopher Columbus flashed back to a childhood memory. It was a memory that he returned to, time and again, when he was challenged or in need of comfort. In his mind, he could hear his teacher's voice as he read from the journals of Marco Polo.

This famous explorer had returned from countless journeys with stories of houses that were capped with golden roofs and sparkling jewels, and palaces that were filled with

121

statues and supported with pillars of solid gold. Such stories filled Christopher Columbus with a yearning for adventure. But some of the stories also fueled his imagination. There were stories of huge gales, blowing from the west that dropped unbelievable things on the shores of Santo Porto. Things like carved timbers of unknown wood. Lengths of bamboo that were so big, their hollow interior could hold gallons of wine. And bodies of yellow skinned people of Asia had also been blown ashore.

Blown ashore from the west! Columbus always exclaimed. *From the west! Certainly they could not blow to Santo Porto from nowhere!*

Christopher Columbus also believed that it was not foolish to believe in places that have never been seen by his own people. After all, most people believed in Heaven–and yet, they have not seen it. And even the Canary Islands were not known until recently. *Surely,* he reasoned, *there are other lands that are yet to be discovered!*

HUMBERTO HAD already gained consciousness and had limped his way back to the helm when Christopher Columbus, Johnny Vic and Dr. Bloom rescued Flesco from his trap. They were still catching their breath when Humberto yelled that they were almost ready to dock.

While they were busy tying off, Johnny Vic caught Dr. Bloom's attention. "We gotta get out of here, Dr. B.! The timer's going to run out in three minutes! They scrambled away, and just before the timer went off, Johnny showed Dr. Bloom his find.

Could that be one of his first attempts at map making? There is no record of his work at such a young age. He was still shaking his head when the air exploded and he felt himself floating.

***

Chapter 15

Home again

Dr. Bloom was still wondering what to think of his amazing dream. *It was a dream, wasn't it?* He scratched his head. He rubbed his chin. He pursed his lips, then he dismissed the entire adventure as an amazing feat of the mind. He suddenly realized he was not alone. Johnny Vic was staring at him.

"Are you okay, Dr. Bloom?"

"I think so. I think so. I'm not sure how I came to be here on the patio, although I suspect I was dreaming and sleepwalking. And I must say, it was a delightfully realistic adventure, this dream of mine. And you were in it, Johnny Vic. Why, we saw Christopher Columbus!"

"Really?"

"Most certainly so."

"Cool."

"Yes. I'll have to tell you about it some day." Dr. Bloom's voice trailed off. He was staring at an object that Johnny Vic was clutching. It looked like a scrap of parchment.

"What do you have there, young man?"

"Me? What do I have?"

"Yes. Right there in your hand. It looks like ancient parchment."

"Oh, this. Well, it's, umh . . ."

Dr. Bloom snatched the fragile fragment from Johnny Vic's hand. It was a crude drawing of the ancient coast of Genoa.

"Johnny Vic! This was in my dream! How could you possibly have . . . Where did it come . . .?" The amazed doctor was suddenly facing the impossible. He was still sputtering with disbelief when Ben appeared.

"What's up, you two? I've been looking all over for you. Did you take a walk? Mrs. Johnson's here to share breakfast with us."

Johnny Vic snatched the opportunity to get away. He rushed into the living room and exclaimed, "Hi, Mrs. Johnson. Eks-KYOOZE me, but we have a very good eks-KYOOSE for being late!"

Dr. Bloom bounced through the door to add, "We were being sub-JECTED to a rigorous hands-on study of a remarkable SUB-ject."

THE END

Facts to Remember

1. Vermont is known as the Green Mountain State.
2. In 1609, Samuel de Champlain became the first non-native to discover Lake Champlain.
3. The Lake Champlain Maritime Museum is a real museum in Vergennes, Vermont.
4. The Lois McClure is a full-scale replica created from the study of two 1862-class sailing canal schooners.
5. Sailing canal schooners carried cargo on Lake Champlain in the 1800's.
6. The canal connecting Lake Champlain to the Hudson River was completed in 1823.
7. An archeologist is a scientist who studies cultures by excavating and examining remains & artifacts.
8. Phosphorus is used to make phosphate fertilizers for plants and is a necessary constituent in plants & animals.
9. Phosphorus pollutes Lake Champlain.
10. Phosphorus makes the lake water become soupy green with algae.
11. Point source pollution enters a body of water from a known source, like pipes and sewer lines.
12. Non point source pollution enters a body of water in runoff from fields, roads, lawns, and gardens.
13. 90-percent of the phosphorus in Lake Champlain comes from non-point sources.
14. Non-point phosphorus pollution can enter the lake from sources that are dozens of miles away.
15. Phosphorus does not break down like some other forms of pollution.
16. The Champlain basin encompasses some 8,200 square miles.
17. Governor Douglas' administration initiated the Clean and Clear Water Plan.

18. The 400th anniversary, known as the Quadricentennial, of Samuel de Champlain's discovery of Lake Champlain occurs in 2009.

19. Champ is a monster that many people claim to have seen swimming in Lake Champlain.

20. The Old Fort House Museum, also known as the Smyth House, is located in Fort Edward, New York.

21. In his farewell address to the nation, President George Washington said that to be successful, religion and morality must be in politics.

22. There were more than 150 Founding Fathers in America–they signed the first major documents, and were very active within the government, but many have not been formally recognized.

23. Squire Ferris, the son of land-owner Peter Ferris, was a 14-year-old boy who witnessed the Battle of Valcour.

24. Benedict Arnold was commissioned by Congress to build 15 warships.

25. On May 10, 1775, about a year and a half before the Battle of Valcour, Benedict Arnold and Ethan Allen & the Green Mountain Boys captured Fort Ticonderoga without firing a single shot.

26. The colonists took control of Fort Crown Point and Skenesborough around the same time that they captured Fort Ticonderoga.

27. Ferris Bay, on Lake Champlain, was the scene of the Battle of Valcour.

28. The chemicals that scientists use to test for phosphorus pollution will turn the water sample blue when they react to the presence of phosphorus.

29. Phosphorus takes oxygen out of water.

30. The Battle of Valcour took place on October 11, 1776.

31. Benedict Arnold and his surviving men escaped from the British by muffling their oars with rags and sneaking away while it was dark.

32. The Colonists lost the Battle of Valcour, but they did manage to cripple the British fleet, forcing them to retreat back to Canada.

33. The Battle of Valcour allowed the Americans enough time to build up their forces before the British could attack them again.

34. Lake Champlain was recognized as the sixth great lake on March 6, 1998, with Senate Bill number 927, but Congress rescinded the proclamation because of demands from politicians from other regions of the country.

35. The Americans had 15 ships and Britain had 25 ships at the Battle of Valcour.

36. The Americans lost 11 ships and about ten percent of their men during the Battle of Valcour.

37. Colonel Guy Carleton was the British Commander at the Battle of Valcour.

38. Colonel Carleton had hoped to divide the American Colonies in half, but the Battle of Valcour stopped him from succeeding.

39. If Benedict Arnold had not stopped Colonel Carleton, the British would have gained control of the Champlain Basin and the Hudson River Valley.

40. The Battle of Valcour was generally regarded as the first naval battle fought by the U.S. Navy.

41. Dorset, Vermont, is the home of one of the first marble quarries of the region.

42. Uncle Sam was created in 1812, because the initials U.S. were printed on crates filled with supplies for the U.S. Army in Troy, New York.

43. White pine was used to create the decks of schooners in the 1800's.

Important Facts to Remember, Continued

44. White spruce was used to create the masts and booms of schooners in the 1800's.
45. White oak was used to create the hulls of schooners in the 1800's.
46. Sailing canal schooners could carry up to 120 tons of cargo.
47. Sailing canal schooners were almost 90 feet long.
48. Sailing canal schooners carried goods, or cargo, on Lake Champlain during the 1800's.
49. Heteronyms are words with the same spelling, but have different pronunciations.
50. Homophones are words that sound the same, but have different spellings & meanings, like ate & eight.
51. A neurosurgeon is a doctor who operates on the central, peripheral nervous system, (including the brain) and some spinal column work.
52. A playwright, is a person who writes plays.
53. Christopher Columbus was also known as Cristobal Colon by the Spanish and Cristofero Colombo by the people in Genoa.
54. Christopher Columbus made four famous journeys to the 'New World.'
55. Columbus and his men were marooned on the north shore of the island country that we now call Jamaica, during their fourth voyage.
56. The Vikings 'hopped' from one land mass to another, including the Shetlands, Iceland, Greenland, and Vineland.
57. Until Columbus made his famous journeys of 2,600 miles or so, the average trip was about 800 miles, often to the Canary Islands.
58. Columbus sailed the ocean blue in 1492.
59. Cassiopeia is a constellation consisting of five stars that form a large, widened W in the sky.

60. Christopher Columbus was marooned in the year 1503, during his fourth voyage.

61. Christopher Columbus had a friend, Spaniard Diego Mendez, who with some natives, sailed a rigged up canoe to Hispaniola to get help for the men in Jamaica.

62. Bartolomeo, the brother of Columbus, sailed with him on his fourth great voyage.

63. Diego Mendez sailed through 40 leagues of treacherous waters in his canoe to get help.

64. Comendador Don Nicolas deOrando, who was in charge of Hispaniola, despised Columbus and waited several months before he sent assistance.

65. On February 29, 1504, Christopher Columbus used his knowledge of an eclipse of the moon to trick hostile natives.

66. Christopher Columbus was born in 1451, in Genoa, Italy.

67. Columbus named a settlement (at what is now known as Haiti) "Navidad" which is Spanish for Christmas.

68. Columbus was named after Saint Christopher, the protector of travelers.

69. King Ferdinand and Queen Isabella ordered the people of Palos to give Columbus three ships for his first voyage: The Santa Maria, the Pinta and the Nina.

70. The Santa Maria was shipwrecked on Christmas Eve in 1492, during the 1st great voyage of Columbus.

71. Columbus named the island of San Salvador after Jesus.

72. In October of the year 1500, Christopher Columbus and two of his brothers were put in chains and returned to Castile by the order of the Kind and Queen.

73. Columbus retained a friendship with Bartolomeo Fieschi (Flesco), whose family was powerful for 200 years or so, and included 50 cardinals and 2 Popes.

Important Facts to Remember, Continued

74. A pomegranate is a fruit that was popular in Genoa.

75. Columbus was inspired by the voyages of Marco Polo.

76. Christopher Columbus died on May 20, 1506.

77. A spectrophotometer is an instrument that measures how much phosphorus is in water.

78. Poignant, (pronounced poin-yant), means keenly distressing, to the feelings.